Thrown to the Wind

Other Books by Amanda M. Cetas

A Home in the Wilderness
At the Mercy of the Sea (forthcoming)

A Country for Castoffs
Book 1

Thrown to the Wind

Amanda M. Cetas

Windy Sea Publishing, LLC

Thrown to the Wind

Book 1 of the Series,
Country of Castoffs
Windy Sea Publishing, LLC

New Edition Copyright © 2023
Copyright © 2019 by Amanda M. Cetas

ISBN-13: 978-1-7332034-0-1 E-Book
ISBN-13: 978-1-7332034-3-2 Amazon
ISBN-13: 978-1-7332034-4-9 Special color edition
ISBN-13: 978-1-7332034-5-6 Ingram

Library of Congress Control Number: 2019910110

Editor: Adriana R. King, Fantastic Literary Services
Cover Design by nskvsky

Author Image: Jim Irish, 2019

Publisher: Windy Sea Publishing, LLC: Tucson, Arizona
www.windyseapublishing.com

Dedication

This story is dedicated to Adriana, who was a constant support and encouragement, and whose insights were invaluable in revising and completing this work and to my father, who pushed me to finish it.

To my mother, sons, brother, sister, nephews and nieces, I hope you will enjoy learning a little more about our family history and the struggles our ancestors endured.

Note

While this is a work of fiction, the people encountered, and the major events described are true to the historical records uncovered. While the personalities are made up, I have tried to do justice to the real people portrayed in this story.

Map on next two pages: *1814 Thomson Map of the Atlantic Ocean*, Public Domain

ATLANTIC
OR
WESTERN OCEAN

Contents

Part 1, The Flight

October 3, 1660

La Rochelle, France

… the Angels hasted Lot, saying, Arise, take thy wife and thy two daughters which are here, lest thou be destroyed in the iniquity of the city. — Genesis 19:15

La Rochelle, The Harbour Entrance, by Jean Baptist Camille Corot
The Yorck Project (2002)

Amanda M. Cetas

Chapter 1

Musketeers

The city was busier than usual and yet there was an uneasy expectancy, like when Papa and I were waiting for my sister to be born. Though at first, nothing looked amiss. Peasants in tattered trousers, rolled sleeves and wide-brimmed hats pushed or pulled carts loaded with crops to sell at market. Fishermen in woolen caps and vivid scarfs carried heaping baskets on their backs from their dinghies to the fish stalls. Servant women hurried from one market stand to the next, baskets brimming with produce and flowers for the fine houses.

What stood out were the numerous noblemen, like exotic peacocks in their brightly colored plumage fringed in lace and topped in feathered hats. These noblemen were all striding purposely toward the cathedral square where the cardinal in his crimson robes stood amidst Jesuit priests milling about like crows searching for crumbs.

The merchants clad in their somber breeches, jackets and capes, and unadorned hats stood in small groups outside their shop fronts talking in hushed tones and glancing uneasily at the collecting noblemen.

I could feel the unevenness of the cobblestones through my worn soles as I hurried on toward the harbor. One stocking had slipped down, but I dared not stop to fix it, for fear of being trampled by the activity in the square.

"Etienne! Watch where you're going."

I looked over my shoulder to see François glaring at me.

"Sorry, I didn't see you."

"You should be sorry *prolé*! You nearly splashed water onto my new shoes and stockings."

My body tensed, and I took a steadying breath. What would he make me do now?

"Go on your way, I don't have time for you today."

That was all I needed to hear. I ran, continuing my circuitous path narrowly dodging a carriage pulled by four horses. François! He was acting strange today. To just let me go without having to grovel at his feet ... something was definitely out-of-sorts today.

I listened for the sounds of the harbor — a few merchants bartering with their customers, while sailors and cavaliers told their tales of adventure, but all was still. It was oddly quiet for the number of people crowding around. Only the smell was the same, that of salt-water, stale fish, and sewage mingling in the breeze.

I was going to meet my cousin Nicolas. We looked like brothers with our mothers' large blue eyes so incongruous with our dark, unruly manes. But Nicholas had a handsome face with broad shoulders and a muscular build. I looked like the awkward little brother, all gangly arms and legs with knobby joints. We were of similar height, though I was only nine; Nicolas was already ten.

He had left me a message, a simple blue ribbon tied to the railing of the garden gate between my house and our landlady's. I knew it must be important. I found him standing by the low wall that skirted the harbor.

Nicolas wore deep blue breeches over white stockings, with a jacket to match and a wide white collar. His feathered hat was the same deep blue with a wide red band, matching the bows on his polished shoes. I suddenly became conscious of my own worn black breeches, dirty jacket and unpolished shoes.

Nicolas smiled and came to embrace me.

"Cousin, I've just heard that the king is sending musketeers here to La Rochelle. They're supposed to arrive today. Everyone is gathering to see them!" Nicolas said.

Nicolas and I had often dreamed of becoming musketeers. They were the elite of the king's soldiers, skilled with sword and musket, or so Nicolas had told me. I'd never seen one.

"Why are they coming here?"

"Father says they're coming to ensure the peace. The cardinal will be making an announcement today on behalf of the king, and he does not want any trouble."

My *père* had once told me that no good would ever come from a military presence in La Rochelle, but he was just an old man. After all, the siege had occurred before Papa was born. Grandfather still remembered it though and never stopped talking about it. The Catholic king, the father of our young King Louis XIV, had tried to prevent the Huguenots, like my *grandpère*, from worshipping in their way. So, the Huguenots rose up in rebellion. The king responded by blockading the city and starving us into submission. After fourteen months, eighty percent of the city's population had died as casualties from fighting, or from plague or famine, including several of Papa's older brothers.

"Look! They're coming. We can see better from up here."

Nicolas leaped onto the wall, and I struggled up after him. The wall was fairly low on the street side, but it was a steep drop on the other side to the docks below. My head began to spin, and I feared I might fall.

"There they are! Magnificent!" Nicolas grabbed my shoulder to steady me, and I looked to where he pointed.

A line of large feathered hats ascended the path from the pier. Slowly they came into view. They *were* magnificent. Their white ruffled shirts shone in contrast to their dark vests, breeches and knee-high, polished boots. White-gloved hands rested on sword handles, gleaming in the light, or supported the butts of muskets leaning against broad shoulders. How I wished I could see one up close. An uneasy hush fell on the crowds as the musketeers filed by us. Nicolas and I watched as they made their way down the street toward the cathedral. As the musketeers moved farther away, the noise of the harbor returned, though it was more subdued than usual.

I looked at Nicolas. I could see the excitement the musketeers brought in his eyes, but his mouth was grim.

"So, was it just the musketeers you wanted to tell me about, or is there more?" I asked, climbing down from the wall.

Nicolas led me away from the crowd along the edge of the pier past the Chain Tower. It was a large round, stone tower that contrasted the angular fortress guarding the opposite side of the mouth of the inner harbor. It got its name for the great chain that could be pulled across to prevent invasion. I supposed it was still there inside, though as far as I knew the Great Siege was the last time it had been drawn. We continued along towards the Lantern Tower, which served as both a lighthouse guarding the mouth of the larger, outer harbor and a prison for pirates and traitors. My cousin leaned in conspiratorially.

"I wanted to warn you. I overheard father talking to the bishop last night. Word has reached him that King Louis XIV is going to crack down on the Huguenot heresy."

I thought of the stories *grandpère* told of the siege and shivered.

"If trouble does come, you can always find shelter with us," Nicolas said.

"What of your father?"

"It's true, my *père* would never openly support your family because of your father's heresy. But my *maman* has always said that she would never turn away her sister, or her sister's children. You would have to get rid of your Huguenot clothing, though, and wear some of mine, but you could easily pass as my brother."

Nicolas stopped and looked at me seriously.

"You saw the numbers of musketeers and soldiers arriving. Why would the king need so many here, if he were not planning something?"

I stared at him mutely. It was true. And, I did *not* want to follow Papa into the stove-making trade. It was hard labor, lifting the stones. I had helped Papa a few times before. I frowned as I remembered the blisters and aching muscles.

"Cousin, I know you want more than your father can ever give you. If you came to live with us, I know Papa … well, I know he would come around and let you stay. And he'd let you take fencing lessons with me. We could both train to become musketeers. Think of it! What fun! What adventures we would have!"

I nodded. I so wanted to become a musketeer. I wanted to be brave and strong like they were. I wanted to be respected and … I took a deep breath to steady my nerves. "Okay. If trouble comes, I will hide with you, until it is safe or, until your father accepts me."

Nicolas clapped me on the back smiling, and, together, we headed back towards the square.

The crowds became thick as we approached the cathedral as everyone in La Rochelle it seemed had turned out to hear the cardinal's announcement.

The cardinal stepped up onto a platform that had been placed there for him in front of the Grand Temple. The building had once been a Protestant church, but the Catholic Diocese of La Rochelle had taken it over after the siege in exchange for the Cathedral of St. Barthélémy, which the Huguenots had destroyed during the siege. They had used the cathedral's bell tower as a gun tower to fend off the king's soldiers, since it stood on the highest point in the city. But even the bell tower was gone now, destroyed by the invading Catholics. The repurposed Grand Temple now served as a constant reminder to those of us Protestants remaining in the city of the power of the king and his Catholic church, and of our failed stance against them. I supposed it was fitting that the cardinal would choose this place to make his announcement.

"Men and women of La Rochelle," the cardinal began as the

crowd fell silent. "King Louis XIV has asked me to announce that he seeks to have unity within his kingdom and within Christendom."

I could hear murmuring from the merchants clustered around the edges of the assemblage.

"To this end," the cardinal continued, "it is the King's desire that the Huguenots within this city convert back to the True Faith. If they do so willingly, then no harm will come to them or to their families. Be it further understood that from this time forward, Protestant Huguenots will no long be allowed to serve in judicial and municipal positions. The courts which formerly held equal numbers of Protestant and Catholic magistrates will no longer do so. All Huguenot seats are to be abolished. Likewise, Protestant craftsmen will be denied the right to practice their trades. And Huguenot members of the Academy of Painting and Sculpture must recant of their heresies or resign their positions."

I could feel the tension rising in the air. Apparently, the musketeers surrounding the cardinal's dais could feel it too as they swung their muskets off of their shoulders in readiness to address any eminent threat.

"Furthermore, pastors are forbidden to perform their duties outside of their place of residence. Protestant worship is also restricted to personal homes. Any Huguenot caught trying to convert anyone to the Protestant heresy will be arrested, as will any Catholic caught trying to convert."

A heavy silence fell over the crowd as the cardinal turned, stepped down from the platform, and retreated up the steps of the converted cathedral. Nicolas put a hand on my shoulder and squeezed. I nodded in response.

"Be safe," he said. "Remember my offer."

I nodded again, unable to speak and watched as he disappeared into the crowd.

Chapter 2

Encounters

I was late! *Maitre Rotund* would whip me for sure. I hurried down the street following the edge of the inner harbor. I ran past the arched façades of the street level shops and the second-story homes, guarded by gargoyles. The last bell chimed as I rounded the corner and saw that the door was closed. Late again! I cringed. I was sure to be the last one, again. *Maitre* would surely notice me. I slowed as I approached the door, trying to catch my breath. Then, as quietly as I could, I slipped in and down the stairs to the basement room, then scurried into my seat on the wooden bench.

The room was lit by a row of small street level windows along the top of one wall. They gave just enough light for our studies but left the room dim, a constant reminder of our unsanctioned status.

"Good of you to join us, Etienne," the schoolmaster said, looking up from his book. "Have you seen Pierre Beaulac? I've not seen him today."

I looked over at Pierre's empty desk. I was not the last! Maybe I would be spared the whip! But where was Pierre? He was usually one of the first to arrive, since he lived just around the corner from the school. In fact, I couldn't remember him ever missing class.

"No, *Maitre* ..." I tried not to flinch as I looked up at the school-master, his large girth straining against his clerical robes. *Maitre* Quintal lived up to his name, which literally meant *Hundredweight*, but I always called him *Maitre Rotund*. Though, I was careful never to say it out loud.

"Very well then. Perhaps he has been detained at home. Now then, John Calvin teaches us that salvation is by faith, not by following the mandates set down by the Catholic Church. He says there is a universal priesthood. What does this mean?"

François's hand shot up first, as usual. "It means that all men should read and interpret the Bible for themselves. We should not need to rely on the corrupted interpretations of the *papists*."

"Very good, François."

I frowned as he flashed me a smug smile. I hated him.

Maitre continued, "We also reject the confession to the priests and pray directly to God for forgiveness. What rule hath God given for our direction in prayer?"

The class recited the catechism in unison, "The whole word of God is of use to direct us in prayer."

"And what is the special rule?"

"But the special rule of direction is that form of prayer which Christ taught his disciples, commonly called *The Lord's Prayer*."

So, I was not going to be whipped. The thought made me smile as I sat with my hands folded quietly on my desk. Pierre's absence had distracted the *maitre* from dispensing the required lashes. What had happened to Pierre? We weren't really friends and never talked together at school; but sometimes, outside of school, we played together. He had been to my house several times, and I had been to his. My papa worked with his father, building stone stoves in the homes of the wealthy nobles. I remembered going to work with Papa several times before my brother, Louis, ... My throat tightened. I swallowed hard and closed my eyes, seeing his small body laid out on the couch, his face, peaceful, as if he were sleeping. I took a deep, shuddering breath and sighed.

After Louis died, I had to stay home to take care of my baby sister, Lidie, while *Maman* spent all day in bed crying. When she got better, Papa and I built a small stove for her. It had made cooking easier, since she didn't have any servants to do it for her. It was the first time she smiled since that ill-favored day. After we had completed the stove for *Maman*, Papa said I needed to be trained in the profession so that, some day, I could take his place. But I didn't want to become a stone-maker merchant. If only there was some other way that I could make up for what I did. I knew that I had no choice. There was no one else. I would have to become a stove-maker like my father. It was hard work hauling the stone. I preferred laying the mortar, but even that was hard work.

"What is the third petition?"

I joined the class in reciting, "*Thy will be done in earth, as it is in heaven.*"

"And what do we pray for in the third petition?"

"That God, by his grace, would make us able and willing to know, obey, and submit to his will in all things, as the angels do in heaven."

Did God want me to be a stove-maker merchant, like my father? I wanted more than that life. I wanted adventure and excitement. I wanted my life to have a purpose. I owed my brother that much.

"Etienne?"

I looked up. Suddenly, I noticed that *Maitre* Quintal and the entire class were watching me.

"If you are ready to rejoin us, we will continue."

I nodded, sheepishly.

"I didn't hear you."

"Yes, *Maitre*." My face burned.

The morning seemed to drag on as we finished reciting our catechism. We took turns reading from the scripture, and then it was time for cyphering. I wished this day would be over. I tried to work on cyphering my arithmetic, but it was hard to concentrate. The numbers didn't make sense. *Maitre* Quintal walked around the room, his footsteps falling heavily on the stone floor.

I imagined myself a musketeer sent by the king to arrest the dreaded pirate Estefan Quintal. He tried to avoid me by darting down a side street, but I was too quick for him. For a moment I lost sight of him as he rounded a corner. I was nearly there. But then ... where did he go? I scanned the street and there ... I saw him. He was trying to kidnap an innocent street boy to crew his dreaded black ship. I drew my sword. He wasn't likely to come easily....

"So how much money would our merchant have left after tithing the church and paying his tax to the king, if he sold four bolts of cloth for 30 Livres a piece? Etienne, give us your answer."

But I didn't have one. The silence grew uncomfortable, and I heard François stifling a laugh behind me.

"Hold out your hand, Etienne," *Maitre* said, looming over me.

I did and squeezed my eyes shut. Crack. His stick came down hard on my hand sending painful prickles radiating through my palm and fingers. I blinked quickly fighting to keep back the tears. I thought back to what the cardinal had announced. By the new law, we were not allowed to attend Protestant school. Maybe he would send his men to arrest *Maitre* Rotund and lock him away in the Lantern Tower *forever*!

The day finally ended, and I left to meet Nicolas. Suddenly, François and his friends, Paul Philippe, Jean, and Jacques, ran by laughing and shoving. As the last one passed, he stuck out a foot, tripping me up. I hit the ground hard. My eyes stung, and my knee hurt. I looked down and noticed that my breeches were torn, and blood was running down my stocking. To make matters worse, I had fallen into the gutter and the stinking refuse was soaking through my clothes.

Maman was going to kill me! I only had three pairs of breeches, one for Sunday, one for school, and one for washing day, and that one was patched and threadbare.

"Look what you did," I yelled after the boys. "You ruined my breeches!"

"Surely, that is not your only pair," François yelled back, and laughed. Then he and his friends rounded the corner, leaving me in the gutter.

Slowly, I stood and walked to Nicolas's house. It hurt to bend my knee. If only I were bigger and stronger, I would make sure they never hurt me again!

"I have something to show you. You won't believe it," Nicolas said, with excitement. "Look at what Papa gave me this morning!"

He was holding a short rapier with a thin, beautifully polished blade. The pummel was an elegant web of iron strips twisted into an airy sphere. The grip was tightly woven dark leather.

"It's beautiful!" I said, trying not to be envious.

"Papa hired a fencing master to teach me how to use it. Do you want to come?"

I nodded, eagerly.

I followed him through the streets to the back entrance of a walled courtyard where the guard recognized him, and grunting, allowed us inside. Several musketeers were also training there. They had removed their large feathered hats and fancy vests as they sparred with one another in the courtyard. But they still looked elegant and imposing in their white, lace-trimmed shirts and finely groomed mustaches.

Nicholas explained all of the moves the musketeers were practicing, excitedly reenacting each parry, repost and lunge with his finger simulating the point of the blade.

"What are you boys doing here?"

The musketeer stood before us looking both impressive and intimidating as he scowled at us, one hand on his sword, the other on his hip. I wanted to shrink into a hole in the ground, but Nicolas thrust out his chin and said, "I brought my cousin here to show him how to fence. I am taking lessons from Master Guillaume de Gaulle."

"I see. Show me what you know then." The musketeer handed him a practice sword and saluted him with a flourish.

Nicolas raised his sword in salute and settled into a fencing stance with his knees bent and right foot leading. The duel was over in a matter of a few quick movements that I could hardly even see.

"You have made a good start, young master. Keep practicing and before long we may wish to recruit you as a musketeer." The musketeer's mouth quirked in a wry smile.

"*Oui*, Sir. I will." Nicolas's face beamed with pride.

Looking across the courtyard a small man in a padded jacket and armed with a wooden sword paced impatiently. Nicolas spotted him too.

"I am late! I am sorry, Sir, but I must go," Nicolas said and hurried to meet the fencing master.

The musketeer laughed low in his throat and turned to me.

"And now you, my young Huguenot. It is unusual to find a Huguenot here in this place. But then you are not ordinary, are you?" He studied me as I shifted my feet. What did he mean that I was not ordinary? I knew that there was nothing unusual about me — nothing special or unique.

"Do you know why we have been stationed here?"

I shook my head and stared at my feet, afraid to meet his eyes.

"We are here to ensure that your lot does not revolt again. Do you know what happened?"

"I know of the sea wall built to prevent aid from coming to the city."

"Do you know why the king laid siege to the city?"

"*Grandpère* told me that the Huguenots were being attacked by the papists."

The musketeer watched me for a moment and asked, "Did you know that the Huguenots destroyed the Catholic relics, burned the crosses, and decimated the saints? Protestants attacked Catholics and many people died on both sides. The Protestant British King, Charles I, tried to come free the city, but in his overconfidence, he failed to bring enough ships. And so the city was very nearly destroyed."

"*Grandpère* said it was the Catholics who brought the trouble to the city." I paused. Was that why we did not openly associate with *Maman*'s Catholic family? Was that why she never spoke to her parents and siblings? How much she must have given up marrying Papa!

"Afterwards, the king mercifully continued to allow religious freedom under the standing terms of the Edict of Nantes, but it appears that his son is not so magnanimous. The era of tolerance is ending. So, we were ordered here, to keep the peace." The musketeer paused and looked at me. "But surely, you would not rebel against our Great Sovereign King, would you?"

"No, Sir, never! In truth, I would also like to join the musketeers someday."

"Would you now? Well then, let us see what you can do." He handed me the practice sword.

"I am sorry, Sir. I have had no training in sword play."

"I dare say that your father would not be pleased to see you here, eh?"

All I could do was stare at the ground. I felt my face flushing. Would Papa care if I studied fencing? I had never considered that he might disapprove, but then I had never asked.

"Don't fear, my young Huguenot. I will not tell anyone of our practice today. Come, I will show you some basic moves, while your friend here has his lesson with Master Guillaume de Gaulle."

My legs and sword arm ached long before we were through, but I would not trade it for anything. It was exhilarating! I wanted nothing more than to return again for more training.

Just before we left, the musketeer slipped something into my hand and said, "A token, to remember this day."

It was a roughly carved wooden musketeer.

I reached the steps to my house. It was a row house, like all the others, but with blue and white tiles covering the façade, instead of the plain white plaster that was typical. I started up the steps, and a sharp pain in my knee nearly brought me down. In the excitement of the afternoon I had forgotten all about my injury. The scab on my knee had stuck to my breeches and pulled open with the movement. It was now bleeding again. I gripped the railing tightly and gritted my teeth as I continued up the stairs.

As I opened the door, I saw Papa carrying a large trunk out of the kitchen. His dark hair had pulled free of its binding and hung over his eyes. Papa's large, broad build filled the narrow hallway. He was red-faced and out-of-breath. He set the trunk down heavily. His dark eyes had a wild look in them.

"We need to go! Now! Pack only what you absolutely need."

Chapter 3

Changes

I stared at Papa incomprehensibly. What did he say? Going? Where were we going? How long would we be gone? I didn't want to believe it.

"Now, *Garçon*! Hurry and pack."

Papa always called me *garçon*, boy. Some people used the term in a derogatory way, to put someone down, or assert their superiority, but I knew Papa used it as a term of endearment. I followed Papa upstairs to the bedroom where *Maman* was lying in bed with my newest baby sister. She didn't have a name yet. She wouldn't be given one until the christening.

"What is the matter, Husband? What has happened?"

Maman was talking to Papa anxiously, but I couldn't hear what they were saying. My father was also named Etienne. I was named for my father, who was named for his father, my *grandpère*. Sometimes I wished they had named me something else.

I stood rooted to the floor, watching my parents talking in hushed tones.

Maman looked so petit in contrast to Papa's broad shoulders and tall stature. Their voices rose; had they forgotten I was here?

"But Husband, the *bèbè* is only five days old! How can we travel now?"

"We have no choice. Since the king's men closed the shop, I can't find any work. No one will hire a Protestant. They arrested Brother Beaulac last night when he went out to protest the king's orders. Brother Rochenfort was arrested this morning for allegedly trying to convert Catholics. *Maitre* Quintal, too, has just been arrested."

They arrested Pierre's papa? That must be why Pierre didn't come to school today. And *Maitre* ... I thought about my wish that he be arrested, and I cringed. It was my fault, just like it was with Louis ... I never should have wished that he would be arrested. But I hadn't really meant it! And I never should have left Louis either. Louis shouldn't have died for my mistake. It should have been me instead. I was no good to anyone, no good at all!

"There's a bounty on my head. I must leave tonight."

The urgency in Papa's voice brought me back. I watched him sit on the bed and stroke *Maman*'s golden-brown hair. "If they take me, what will happen to you and the children?"

"But where will we go?" *Maman* asked.

"Brothers Lefévre and Richelieu have arranged passage for as many of us as want to leave for Amsterdam. Brother Richelieu's bank has business connections there. It is a large trade city, and the Dutch are Calvinists too. We will be safe there."

Papa said that François's father had made the arrangements. I sighed. The only thing worse than having to leave La Rochelle, was having to go with François!

"We have already lost one son, and the *bèbè* is so small. I can't ..." *Maman* looked down at my sleeping sister, then her blue eyes looked into Papa's dark ones. "Perhaps my sister could take us in? Maybe her husband would protect us?"

"Do you really believe that? You know that he holds no love for me or our faith. But, if you prefer to stay, take the children and go to your sister's house. You will have to disavow me. I will send you money, as soon as I can."

Maman was quiet for what seemed like forever and covered her eyes with her hands. Finally, she took a deep breath and said, "We will go with you."

"*Garçon*, we need to go," Papa said, noticing me in the doorway. He walked over and put his large, callused hands on my shoulders. "I need your help tonight. Please, go and help Lidie pack. Then pack your own things. We can't take much, only your clothes and what few things you can carry. We will leave at midnight." Then Papa hurried past me and down the stairs.

My sister Lidie, as the oldest daughter, was named after my mother, Lydia.

Maman motioned for me to sit beside her on the bed. Her voice was soft, but I could hear it trembling. "You must be brave. Papa needs you tonight." She paused and took my hand. "I need you too."

"Where is Amsterdam, *Maman*?"

My mother's blue eyes looked worried, "It is in northern Europe, so you must dress warmly." She pulled herself up to lean against the pillows. She looked like a queen in spite of wearing only her nightgown. I helped her to stand, leaving the baby sleeping on the bed. She always stood so straight and walked so gracefully. She rarely spoke of my grandparents, but I knew that she was the daughter of a noble birth.

"What's wrong with Papa?"

Maman caught me in her arms. "Go. Pack your things, Etienne, there will be time for questions later. Hurry now!"

I sighed and nodded. I couldn't let her and Papa down again. Not after Louis …

Chapter 4

Choices

Lidie was in the attic, which served as our bedroom. She was playing with a doll *Maman* had sewn from old clothes. She was only three years old. I let her play as I took our clothes out of the small wardrobe and folded them on the bed.

"What are you doing?" she asked, looking up at me with her dark eyes.

"Papa said we had to pack our things. We are going to take a trip."

"Where are we going?" she asked excitedly.

"I don't know. It's a surprise."

"Oooh! Can I take Ana?" she asked, holding up the tatty doll.

"*Oui*, of course you can. Now come over here and help me pack your clothes."

It didn't take long to pack up the few things we had. I looked around the room. It was sparse. There were two beds, one on either side of the small wardrobe that occupied the highest point of the wall. The gabbled roof sloped sharply down to touch the floor on either side of the beds. A small woven rug took up the center of the floor. A small window opposite of the wardrobe stood open to let in the breeze. As I walked over to close it, I noticed the nine wooden pins and leather ball stacked neatly beneath it and caught my breath sharply. My heart started thumping, and I froze in my tracks. Louis. It had been my game, but Louis had liked to play with it. I hadn't used it since that day. It was all I had left of him. I carefully picked up the pins and ball, blinking back tears, stuffed them into a small satchel, and I carried them to the trunk opened on the bed. There would be room for these.

After packing, I took Lidie's hand and went downstairs to the kitchen for supper. I sat Lidie on the bench at the table and slid in next to her. I watched *Maman* ladle the pottage, a soup made of ground beans and vegetables, into small wooden bowls. The kitchen was small with a table and benches on one side of the room and the fireplace and stove dominating the other. Strings of garlic and bunches of thyme, chervil, and parsley hung from rafters over the table, giving the room a pungent garden smell. *Maman* set a board loaded with a large chunk of bread, grapes, and nuts in the center of the table. She then poured wine for Papa and herself and wine diluted with water for Lidie and me. We ate in silence.

After supper, we gathered around the fireplace while Papa read from the Bible. It was the story of Daniel in the Den of Lions. Daniel was a young Hebrew, who had been taken from his home in Judah to the city of Babylon, where he was being trained to enter the king's service. He had many enemies at court and they accused him of being disloyal. He was arrested and thrown into the den of lions for refusing to bow down to the Babylonian king. But God closed the mouths of the lions so that they could not eat him.

"Remember, Etienne, my *garçon*, kings derive their power from the people, not from God. Our duty is to serve God first and kings second, no matter what may happen."

"Now off to bed with you both. Papa will wake you when it is time to leave," *Maman* said, softly.

Lidie was sound asleep, making soft snoring noises. I slipped out of bed and dressed quickly. I lifted the satchel with the ball and nine-pins out of the open trunk and slung it over my shoulder. Then I slipped the wooden musketeer figurine into my jacket pocket and tiptoed to the door. For the past hour, I had lain in bed listening to Papa's heavy footfalls as he moved about the house packing all of our necessaries and other valuables for the impending trip from La Rochelle and the only home I had ever known. I thought about the offer Nicholas had made me. If I left La Rochelle now, I would never become a musketeer. I decided that I would stay, so I waited until the house grew quiet.

My hand hovered over the door handle for a moment, and I held my breath as I carefully undid the latch. I started down the steps carefully. I made it halfway down the hallway and heard a loud CREAK! I froze. I heard the baby whimpering and *Maman* singing softly to her.

Would she notice me? I stood there unsteadily with my weight on one foot for another moment. I thought I caught her eye through the cracked door. My stomach lurched. But she continued singing. I realized my eyes were shut. I opened them cautiously. *Maman* was still looking down at the baby. She didn't see me, after all. I continued by and slid down the stair railing, hopping to the floor before I hit the banister. I peered around the corner and saw Papa in the sitting room reading the Bible by candlelight. His back was to me and he seemed not to have heard me. As quietly as possible, I crossed the entryway and slipped out the door.

I made it! I gave a silent victory whoop and added a little bounce to my gait.

There were few people out at this hour. Most were home eating their suppers or were already in bed. I hurried down the cobblestone street toward the docks. As I rounded the corner, the street filled with people and noise. The docks were always busy late into the night. I turned to the right and kept moving until I saw the great towers flanking the mouth of the inner harbor. I cut around a fisherman staggering out of a tavern, and then darted to the left to avoid four sailors struggling with a large barrel.

Nicolas would likely be asleep when I got there. I thought about what to do. Should I bang on the door and make a plea to his father? No, he would likely send me home or report me to the authorities. Nicolas's room is on the second floor of his parents' home overlooking the back garden, but a high wall surrounded it.

I heard a loud bang behind me. I spun around and saw two burly sailors exiting a tavern. They were dragging a man between them. The man appeared to be unconscious. A third sailor was giving orders.

"Get him to the ship. By the time he wakes up, we should be well out to sea."

"What'll we do if he refuses to work?" the smaller sailor asked.

"He'll work. If not, we'll throw 'im overboard."

Cavaliers! Pirates. I shrunk back into the shadows, hoping I would not be noticed. I had heard the stories of pirates kidnapping drunkards and young boys from the streets to crew their ships. Once out to sea the captives had no choice but to serve. La Rochelle was a major port linking France to Africa and the Americas. I knew that once caught, there would be no chance of making it home.

I backed up cautiously, keeping an eye on the pirates, until I finally reached the corner. I slipped around the bend and started running. I was out-of-breath when I finally reached Nicolas's house. Now I stood staring at the large façade.

How wonderful would it be to take fencing lessons with Nicolas! Maybe my uncle would even buy an old sword for me to use. I pictured myself dressed in the fancy garb of a musketeer and smiled. But then I thought of Papa. He would be so disappointed in me. I knew that he would need help getting established in Amsterdam. Who else could help him build the potager's stoves? But I wanted to become a musketeer. I didn't want to be a stove-maker!

I stared up at the house looming before me. There were no candles flickering in the windows. The house was dark. Even the lamp at the front door had been extinguished. I walked around to the garden gate. If Nicolas were expecting me, he would have left it open. I felt my way along the wall, feeling for the brick to give way to wood. There … the wood felt solid, and as I felt along it, I realized that it had been left ajar.

I crept into the garden and looked up at the house. There was a small candle flickering in one window on the second story. That would be Nicolas's room. If I tossed a stone at his window, I knew he would come and let me in. I dropped to my knees and found a suitable one; I rolled it gently between my fingers, hesitating.

If I left, I would likely never become a musketeer. And I might never see Nicolas again. But if I stayed, what would happen to Lidie? I could see her crying when she learned that I had not come home. Could I really do that to her? Besides, Papa would know where I'd gone. I was sure he would come looking for me. Papa had never whipped me, but the consequences would be far worse. Papa would never leave La Rochelle without knowing what had happened to me. And then he might miss the ship. He would be arrested and taken to the lantern tower.

No, I would have to go back. My heart ached, as if someone had sliced it in two. Time seemed to stop as I stood there suspended between two futures. Nicolas had offered me sanctuary and the life I dreamed of, but then Papa …

I closed my eyes and sighed deeply, I slipped the stone into my pocket, turned, and headed home.

Chapter 5

Flight

The street was quiet when we left our house. The darkness felt thick and almost solid, as if it would smother me. Not even the moon had ventured out to light our way. Though Papa wouldn't say where we were going or for how long, I knew it was the last time I would see my home. Papa loaded the trunks into the back of the wagon. He helped *Maman* and the baby, wrapped in a thick bundle of blankets, onto the bench. Then he lifted Lidie into the back of the wagon. I stood there on the steps, unable to move. I rolled the small stone I'd picked up earlier between my fingers as I thought of Nicolas and my promise. When he learned that we were gone, would he think we were arrested, or killed? Or would he feel betrayed that I had just left without honoring my promise … without even an explanation … or a goodbye?

"*Garçon*, hurry!"

I looked down to see Papa motioning for me to come.

Reluctantly, I let the stone fall from my fingers, and I started down the steps leading to the street. A feeling of dread grew with each step. At the bottom, I stopped and looked back at the blue and white tiled house on Rue Les Cloustiers. It was the only home I had ever known. I looked up at my room in the attic of the little house, just under the steeply pitched clay-tiled roof. I will miss playing in the little garden pressed between our house and the home of our landlady, Madam Georget. Lanterns hung from a few of the homes, beacons warding off the frightful dark.

"*Garçon?*" Then Papa's tone softened, "Hurry into the wagon. Time is short."

I nodded to Papa, climbed into the back of the wagon and sat down next to Lidie on a large trunk. The wagon lurched and bounced down the cobbled street. As we turned a corner, homes gave way to darkened shops hidden beneath a row of arches yawning open like great mouths. I shuddered, imagining all sorts of dragons, manticores and demons lurking in their depths. I wrapped a blanket tighter around my shoulders and tried to look brave. After all, I was nine now and didn't believe in monsters anymore. Then I saw them! Two eyes glowing yellow in the dark. They peered at me from beneath one of the arches. There was movement! A tail brushed aside a crate carelessly, as he prepared to come for me ....

"Where are you off to at this hour?" A man yelled, hurrying out onto the street. "Haven't you heard that a curfew has been ordered?"

The horse lurched, as Papa spurred him to run faster.

"Come back! I'll have you reported!"

The horse rounded the corner, and the wagon tipped dangerously onto two wheels. I caught my breath, and Lidie grabbed my arm.

Soon, the smell of fish and salt reached out to suffocate me. I had been to the docks many times before, but never in such darkness, never like this. We were met by a trollish-man, carrying a lantern. He helped Papa with the trunks and led us down to a small boat tied up along the dock. The water of the harbor looked like obsidian. I tried not to imagine the horrors that might lie beneath its dark surface. I felt Lidie scoot closer, clinging to my arm. I freed my arm and wrapped it around her, and she snuggled in close. Slowly, we were rowed out into the mist. No one spoke.

Gradually, the harbor towers came into view, rising out of the fog, great shadows guarding the inner harbor. Their presence was felt more than seen. I held my breath as we passed between them and prayed the guards patrolling around the top parapets would not see us. I wasn't sure why we should not be seen, only that it was absolutely necessary that we were not. Out in the larger harbor we passed by several large ships until, finally, we pulled up alongside one anchored in the deep water. Two sailors tied our trunks to ropes, while others on deck hoisted them up. Then they helped *Maman* up the rope ladder to the deck. I went up next, followed by a sailor carrying Lidie, and another carrying the baby. Papa came up last.

Once on board, we were led below deck to the cargo hold. Boxes and barrels loomed over us on both sides, stacked from floor to ceiling. The ship rocked back and forth causing us to stagger like the drunken sailors I'd seen earlier. All it would take was one person stumbling into some of the barrels to bring the whole lot down on our heads.

It got darker as we moved deeper into the ship's belly. A small space opened up and our trunks were dropped heavily into a growing pile of other trunks, crates, and barrels. And then we were shown to a trap door leading down to a second hold. This lower hold was already full of other people sitting on the rough wooden floor. Papa had to walk hunched over to avoid hitting his head on the rafters. Our guide held an oil lantern, the only light in the place. Eyes glowed, staring at us as we passed. Finally, Papa was shown a small space at the rear of the hold. After helping *Maman* and my sisters onto a folded quilt he had laid down for them, he sat down on the wooden floor and motioned for me to join him.

The man with the light left. A baby cried from somewhere in the dark and was quickly hushed. It was too quiet for so many people in such a cramped space.

The silence seemed to swallow us. My chest felt tight; I felt a tear escape and tasted the salt on my tongue. I was thankful for the dark. Only babies cry. I wasn't a baby anymore. I reached into my pocket and squeezed the small wooden figure the musketeer had given me, for good luck.

"It will be alright *Garçon*. God will provide," my father said, gently, as if he sensed my thoughts. "Go to sleep now. Everything will look better in the morning."

But it wouldn't. I knew it wouldn't. I didn't even know where we would be when we woke up.

Chapter 6

Escape

I couldn't sleep. I heard voices on the deck. The rocking of the ship was almost soothing, but I couldn't stop thinking about Nicolas. I put my hand in my pocket and slowly traced the contours of the little musketeer. Nicolas was my best and really, only friend, in the world. I already loved him as a brother. To become his actual brother, would be the most natural of things.

The ship was still anchored. It would be no great effort to drop overboard and swim to shore. The Lantern Tower would show the way. Then I could go to Nicolas.

"Where are you going?" Papa asked me.

"Nowhere. I just can't sleep."

"Think of a happy memory, or a Bible story, and try to relax."

I sat in the dark listening to Papa's breathing. I could feel the ship pulling at its anchor, wanting to be released, just like me. A baby cried again, and I heard suckling. The air was stifling, stagnant. I pulled off my jacket, but it did no good. Too many people. I had to get out! I listened. Papa's breathing had slowed. It had a rhythmic quality. It was time to go.

Carefully, I crawled forward in the direction where I hoped to find the ladder. It was dark, so dark that I couldn't see my hand in front of my face. The baby had quieted. I heard people all around me stirring, breathing, whimpering. I had to get out! I knew I had made the wrong decision! I just had to get back to Nicolas while there was still time. My heart was beating so fast it felt like it would break out of my body. It was so hard to breathe. A rat chattered at me when I moved too close to it. I continued on feeling my way along the floor.

Suddenly my head cracked into something hard. I tried not to cry out, rubbing the knot forming on my head. I felt around and discovered I had run into the wooden ladder. I climbed the stairs to the deck carefully, so as not to lose my footing in the blackness. The trap door creaked a little as I lifted it, and I froze. No one seemed to have noticed, so I slipped out and set it back in place as quietly as I could. It was a little lighter here. The barrels and boxes filling the hold loomed over me like giants threatening to rip me apart. I had to feel my way between and around them to get to the second ladder. I saw the stars shining down through the open hatch. As I reached the top, I heard voices speaking quietly, but urgently.

"We must get underway."

"Capt'n, it's too dark. How will we safely navigate out of port?"

"We must. If we stay here, it will be too late. The king has ordered all ships in the harbor boarded in the morning. They have been ordered to detain any Huguenots trying to leave. Anyone caught harboring them will be arrested along with them."

"Then why don't we just turn them over?"

"I have no desire to turn these people over to the hangman. So long as we leave port before dawn, we can make it to Holland."

As they moved away, I crept out onto the deck and found a crevice from which I could watch the sailors scurrying about the deck readying the sails and pulling up the anchor. In the distance I saw the light from the Lantern Tower. The light was, both comforting and chilling; a guide for safe travels and a prison for pirates and traitors; a beacon calling me home and warning of impending doom. I wondered if Pierre's father was being held there right now. What if that had been my own father?

There was a clear path to the railing. Then I could slip over and drop into the water. I would swim toward the lighthouse. I might still be able to make it before dawn. The beacon's glow was steady and unwavering, showing the way back to Nicolas. If I was going to jump it would have to be now.

My heart was pounding in my ears. I didn't want to leave La Rochelle, and I didn't want Papa arrested. But he was safe now onboard the ship. What would happen to *Maman* and Lidie and the baby? When my younger brother, Louis, died *Maman* wouldn't come out of her bedroom for weeks. She didn't eat for days. Papa stopped going to work in order to care for her. It was a long time before she came back from that dark place. I knew she wouldn't survive losing Papa. But after what I'd done, would she even notice that I was gone? Would she mourn my absence? Maybe she would be happy? But I knew, in my gut, that she would notice. She would miss me, and Papa couldn't both work and care for her and the girls too. Maybe I should leave her a note, so that she would know that I am safe, so she wouldn't worry? But if I went back down to the hold, I knew Papa would stop me. Maybe I could leave the note in our trunk instead?

The ship began to move, and I saw the Lantern Tower slipping away into the dark. There was still time to leave, but no time for a note. I would have to go now, or not at all. I thought of *Maman* and Lidie and Papa. I sighed. How could I leave them? *Maman* would never know what happened to me. I had failed Louis. How could I fail them again? I would have to stay. We were going to be safe. Except, we wouldn't be home. And I wouldn't see Nicolas ever again.

Suddenly, a cannon was fired, and I heard yelling. Someone hailed the captain.

"I command you to stop, in the name of the king! Prepare for boarding."

Chapter 7

Caught

The deck filled with sailors readying themselves to face the navy. The king's seamen climbed over the side of the ship. They all looked the same to me, even in the light of the lanterns. I could feel the rising tension all around me and pressed back further under the stairs. I caught my breath when someone stomped down from the upper deck. I could see the polished boots through the risers. They came to stop halfway down. Then I saw the sailors move aside to let a tall man approach. He wore a long dark coat lined in gold trim. He came to stand at the foot of the steps.

"Good evening, Captain," the man in the dark coat said.

"What is the purpose of this boarding, Commander?"

"The King has given orders to search all vessels leaving La Rochelle, and to arrest any Huguenots aboard."

"We are a cargo ship. We have no passengers, only what you see here."

"Then you won't mind if we search the ship."

"We are already late leaving port. We were scheduled to leave this morning but had some repairs that took longer than anticipated. A search would hold us up, unnecessarily."

"I presume you are not questioning the purposes of the King?"

"No, only the waste of time to you and me in conducting a search that will turn up nothing."

"I appreciate your desire to get underway, though I question why you don't want to wait for the safety of dawn, which is nearly here. It makes me wonder what you are trying to conceal."

The officer gestured to one of his men and whispered something to him. Then he pointed in my direction. I gasped and pulled back into the shadows, but it was no good. Two sailors hauled me out from under the stairs. I stood unsteadily looking at the deck boards. What would they do with me? Had I endangered my family and everyone else on the ship? I should have just stayed below with Papa.

"What is this boy doing here? Who is he?" The officer's voice was hard, and I dared not answer or raise my head to look at him.

"He is my sister's son. She asked me to train him as a cabin boy. What he is doing here and not in his hammock, I cannot say."

I turned and looked up at the captain. His eyes were stern, and I quickly dropped my eyes again. As the silence became awkward, I realized he was waiting for me to say something.

"I wanted to see what the commotion was about?" I said, trying to keep my voice steady.

"Well, now that you are here, you can escort me as we show this officer below decks."

I nodded and dared to look at his face. He couldn't be much older than my father, but the years of wind and sun had carved lines in his face. His mouth was set in a hard line, but his eyes softened a little as he acknowledged my compliance.

The captain turned to another man, I thought must be the first mate, and said, "Get me a lantern."

I fell in behind the captain, who led the naval officer and four of his crewmen down the stairs. How could the captain succeed in keeping my family and all the others below hidden? Would he hand them over? What would happen if he did? I tried not to think about it for fear my face would give them away.

The captain took us through the kitchen and food stores first and the bunkroom lined with rows of hammocks used by his crew. The officer was getting impatient by this time, so we returned to the cargo deck. They were sure to see the trap door to the sub-deck. I tried to steady my breathing. The men started moving crates and examining the corners and along the darkened walls. I stood in the center of the room with the captain.

"Where is the door to the lower hold?" the officer asked, walking toward us.

"This is the only cargo hold. Below is just ballast."

"We must be thorough," the officer said, the corners of his mouth twitching.

It was over. They would find my family now.

Chapter 8

Revelation

The captain took my arm and moved me off the trap door. The officer then ordered one of his men to lift the hatch. He stood over the opening holding the lantern as he peered into the darkness. I closed my eyes and prayed. Please, God, protect my family.

"Petyr, come here," the officer said, motioning him with his hand. "Go, see what's down there."

The seaman started down the ladder, slowly. When his head slipped beneath the floor, the officer reached down and handed him the lantern. I watched the light disappear and held my breath. I expected to hear the cries of the women and children being discovered, but all was quiet. He was gone for what felt like hours. My hands were wet and slimy. I wiped them on my breeches.

"What cargo are you carrying? And where are you headed?" the officer asked.

"We brought furs, salted fish, rice and sugar back from the Americas, which were off-loaded here. Then we picked up wine, porcelain tiles, and felt hats in La Rochelle to transport to Holland," the Captain replied.

"Then what are in these other trunks?" The officer swept his arm over the trunks and crates stacked high in the corner.

It was too dark to see them clearly, but I was sure that many of the trunks were stuffed tightly with our personal belongings and those of the others below our feet.

"We are bringing fine silk clothing of the latest fashions for the new elite in Amsterdam. As you know, all of Europe longs to imitate our great taste for such luxuries."

"We shall see."

The officer started to move toward one of the trunks. I knew he would open it, only to find an unfortunate family's belongings and not the finery of nobility. He laid a hand on the top of the trunk and bent to inspect the latch. Just then, the light grew, and the seaman's head popped up through the opening. It no longer mattered what the officer might find in the trunk, there was no way the seaman could have missed all the people stowed like ballast in the depths of the ship.

"All's clear. Just ballast, like the captain says."

"Truly?" the officer said, studying the seaman, thoughtfully. "Well, then, it looks like you are free to leave."

The officer turned and led the way back towards the steps leading up to the deck. As the seaman turned to follow him, I saw him smile slightly, I could swear that he winked at me! The captain put a hand on my shoulder and gently directed me to follow them.

"Take our cabin boy back to my quarters and ensure that he stays there," the captain told his first mate, as he turned to watch the officer and his crewmen leave the ship.

I followed my escort in silence. What would the captain do to me now? We reached the rear of the ship, and the first mate opened a small wooden door. He gestured for me to enter. A large wooden bed was built into the wall on the right side of the room. In the center, stood a large table with maps and charts spread over it. The first mate motioned to one of the wooden chairs surrounding the table. I walked over but refused to sit down. The first mate made a gesture of indifference and held his position at the door. A lantern hung over the table. A wardrobe was built into the wall opposite the bed. Three small windows occupied the back wall. I stared at the maps on the table, but I didn't understand them. Finally, I walked over to the bank of windows and sat down in one of the two padded chairs standing there. I could see the Lantern Tower off to my left. We must be moving, because the bobbing light was shrinking into the distance.

The door opened, and the captain came in. He nodded a dismissal to his first mate. The captain crossed the room in a few long strides and sat in the chair facing me. He had eyes the color of a gathering storm. He was not nearly so tall as my father, of slender build, and delicate features on a weathered face which made him look older than he was. The captain removed his hat revealing blond hair tied neatly back at the nape of his neck.

He was studying me, just as I studied him.

"What is your name?" he asked.

"Etienne," I replied, dismayed to hear my voice crack awkwardly.

"I am Captain Carteret," he said, extending a hand. His grip revealed greater strength than his slender hands suggested. "Do you know how lucky you and the others are?"

I stared at the floor, silently.

"If he had reported seeing your people down there, I would have been forced to hand them over." He paused, and I could feel him staring at me. "You, I might have saved, assuming I wasn't arrested also."

"What good would that do if they had taken my family?" I asked, suddenly angry.

"Don't you think your parents would prefer you to be safe, rather than being killed alongside them?"

"Maybe, but how could I go on knowing they were dead?"

The captain took a deep breath and sighed. "We all have to live with difficult things. It is fortunate that I did not have to give them up tonight, but we are not out of danger yet. The Navy patrols the waters along the French coast all the way up to the English Channel. They may yet stop us. I need you to stay with the others below decks until I send word that you can come up. Will you do that for me?"

I nodded. My face flushed. How could I have been so stupid? I wiped away a tear before the captain could see it.

Captain Carteret stood and put his hand on my shoulder.

"Do your parents know where you are?"

I shook my head.

"Then you had best get back to them." The captain escorted me to the door. "Now get some sleep."

"*Oui.*"

When I crawled up next to Papa, he embraced me and whispered, "Where have you been? I was worried about you, and when we saw the light … we thought we would be arrested and never see you again!"

"I'm sorry, Papa. I went up to the deck to look around. I was thinking about Nicolas."

An awkward silence enveloped us.

"Papa, why do we have to leave?" I whispered.

"The king has outlawed many of the practices of our faith, calling us heretics. He has put a bounty on my head and on many other known Protestants. If we don't leave now, I will surely be arrested on the morrow, and executed soon after."

"Why, Papa? What did you do?"

"Nothing."

"I don't understand why the king cares what faith we follow."

"Because we have rejected the corruption of the Catholic Church. We fight for religious tolerance in order that we may follow our conscience unmolested. The king sees that as a threat. We are not being wholly loyal to him and the Catholic Church."

"Is that why you didn't want me to go to the Latin grammar school with Nicolas, because you don't like Catholics?"

"I don't dislike Catholics, but I don't subscribe to everything the pope decrees, and I wanted you to be taught the truth."

"I understand why the king thinks we could be a threat. The Huguenots did lead a rebellion before. But I still don't understand why the Catholics care what we practice."

"It's all about power. The Catholic Church has developed a hierarchy built upon controlling the doctrines and practices of the faith. The Catholic Church views the pope as infallible. But we believe that he blasphemes God by claiming His authority. And so, any doctrine that counters the pope is deemed as heresy and a threat to his authority. The papists convinced the King that we are dangerous. They cry out for our destruction. That is why we must leave."

"When will we be able to come home?"

"I don't know, *Garçon*. Go to sleep. Everything will look better in the morning."

I laid there in the dark feeling the warmth of Papa against my side and listening to his steady breathing, until, finally, sleep found me.

Chapter 9

Betrayed

On the second day of our voyage, after determining that the Royal Navy was not following us, Captain Carteret had finally let us come up on deck. It was warm for October; the smell of salt water was refreshing compared to the human stench permeating the lower decks. Even *Maman* and Papa had suffered from seasickness ever since we had left the relative calm of the harbor and entered the tumultuous Atlantic Ocean.

The first mate had opened the hatch above where we were hiding and lowered a lantern, which he hung on a hook by the open hatchway.

"The captain says it is safe to come up to the deck now. The sun and fresh air may do you good."

I moved to help *Maman* up, but she waved me away.

"Maybe later, Etienne. You go."

I looked at Papa. He nodded and brushed me aside, grabbed a bowl and vomited into it. I left them and scrambled up the ladder, hurried across the cargo hold and up the second ladder into the fresh air. I stood on the deck breathing deeply and feeling the wind on my face.

A group of boys was forming a few paces away from me. I knew them. Jean Guenon, Jacques Cousseau, and Paul Philippe Richelieu from school. Tomas Lefévre was there too. He was two grades below me, and he was François's brother. Jean and Jacques were cousins, both of them fair-haired. Their fathers were dealers in silks and the blue and white porcelain from the Orient. Paul Philippe was the tallest in the class, standing head and shoulders above all of us. His father was a banker. It was his business connections in Amsterdam and Brother Lefévre's shipping contacts that had set us all on this dismal adventure to Holland. Tomas was timid and frail-looking with light brown hair and eyes that were too large for his face. He was nothing like his bully of a brother. I looked around. François was nowhere to be seen. I wanted to join them, but I hesitated.

The boys seemed to be arguing. As I watched, trying to decide whether to go over or not, I saw Paul Philippe gesturing in my direction; I hesitated. These boys had never been nice to me, but, maybe without François, it would be different. I got up and walked over.

"Hey, Etienne, do you want to play with us? We are playing Pirates and King's Men."

"Sure."

"Good, we need someone on the Pirates' side."

"Okay."

"You can team up with Jean and Jacques. I'll team with Tomas," Paul Philippe said.

I nodded to Jean and Jacques.

"Since you guys are the Pirates, you get a head start to the count of ten," Tomas announced. In an instant, Jean and Jacques took off, leaving me standing on the deck, stunned. Quickly, I started to follow as they disappeared below decks.

I climbed down the ladder and squinted into the darkness waiting for my eyes to adjust. They were nowhere to be seen. I called out for them, and then I heard the others talking at the top of the ladder and dove behind a large crate, nearly landing on top of Jacques. He grunted an obscenity and made room for me. Jean motioned us to silence.

The King's Men made a big pretense of searching for us. Then, as they drew near, Jean grabbed me, and Jacques popped up yelling, "Over here!"

Suddenly, I found myself being dragged out of my hiding place. I caught my breath as I saw François standing before me flanked by Tomas and Paul Philippe.

"You have been charged with piracy and high treason against the Crown," François bellowed in an authoritative voice. "Guards, take him!"

"I surrender," I said, raising my hands. I expected the game to be over. Instead, Pierre and Tomas led me over to a large barrel stowed beneath the stairs and tied my hands behind my back with a bit of twine. Then François opened the top of the barrel and forced me to get into it. He replaced the lid, and I heard something heavy land on top.

"Now we will leave you to think about your crimes." I recognized the voice as François's.

"What crimes?" I asked, loudly, trying to be heard.

"The crime of being a pirate and a *prolé*."

"My father is a merchant, just like yours!"

The boys laughed.

"Your father is not like mine," François said loudly. "My father is a wealthy merchant. We buy furs from America and silks from China. We employ dozens of tailors and hat makers to clothe the nobility. Your father is a *prolé*, a manual laborer."

"Let me out. This isn't fun anymore."

"Let you out? Certainly not! Not until you have paid for your crimes."

I could hear the boys moving away and pressed my ear to the slats in the barrel, straining to hear more.

"François, we can't just leave him here." It sounded like Tomas, François's younger brother. "We should untie him now."

"We'll let him sit a bit first. Come on Tomas."

I heard the boys retreating and thought back to the first day I started at the Protestant school. My mother had made my jacket, instead of buying one from the tailor, so though it was similar to the ones worn by the other students, it was not the same. I remembered hearing the snickers and whispers as I took my seat. Yes, it was true. I have always known that we were different — different from my Catholic family, different even from our Protestant community.

I waited, expecting the boys to come back. I heard the seamen on the deck talking in muffled tones as they worked. I heard the creaking of the ship and muted groans from below.

It was common for sons to follow in the professions of their fathers. François would become a fur merchant someday inheriting his father's business and Paul Philippe would become a banker, but I didn't want to build stoves. I thought of Papa's rough, calloused hands. They were strong hands; they were hands that have always worked hard. But they could also be gentle. I remembered how tenderly Papa held Lidie after she was born and how patiently he cared for *Maman* … how they trembled when they held my brother on that day, four years ago …

"Take your brother to the garden, son. I need to rest."

"But, Maman, I was just going to see Nicolas."

"Not today."

"But he is expecting me…."

"No, not today. I need you to watch Louis."

I watched Maman suckling Lidie a moment longer and frowned angrily. I took Louis by the hand and dragged him downstairs to the small garden wedged between our house and Madam Georget's. I set up nine wooden pins and gave Louis the small leather ball. Why did I always have to watch my brother? Every time I had something planned with Nicolas, I had to watch my brother! I watched him clumsily throw the ball at the pins, trying to knock them down. He missed and ran after the ball. I hoped this game would keep him busy for a while.

"Hey, Etienne."

I looked up to see Pierre Beaulac standing in the back alley behind the railing.

"Hi."

"Sorry about François. He thinks because his father is head of the fur traders' guild, he is better than everyone else."

I nodded. "Would you like to play nine pins with me? We'll have to let my little brother play too."

"I can't right now. A group of us are going to watch the boats come into the harbor. Do you want to come?"

I looked over at Louis. His face was scrunched up in concentration, and his tongue stuck out of the side of him mouth, as it always did when he was focused. I was sure that he wouldn't miss me.

"Okay, sure."

Pierre smiled. "Great. Do you need to take your brother too?"

"He'll be okay. The game should keep him busy for a while," I said, opening the low gate and stepping through. We started walking down the street towards the harbor. I heard the clopping of horse hooves striking the cobbled stones behind us.

"Are you sure your brother will be alright by himself?" Pierre asked.

I felt a guilty pang and turned around just in time to see Louis climbing the low fence surrounding our garden.

"Wait for me!" Louis yelled, running toward me.

"Louis!" I took off running, but before I could cover the distance to the fence, he ran into the road. It was over by the time I reached him. The driver tried to stop, but the carriage was going too fast, and the road was slick.

I could still see him lying there in the street when I closed my eyes. The driver had gone for a doctor, while one of the passengers, a nobleman dressed in his finery, had carried my brother's broken body into the house.

I thought of Papa again. He had stayed home with *Maman* for two weeks after the incident, comforting and caring for her. Though, I re-membered once hearing him mourning Louis quietly, alone in the sit-ting room long after everyone else was supposed to be asleep. I knew Papa would do anything for *Maman*. He would never let her down.

I felt a tear escape and roll down my check. I tasted the saltiness on my tongue. The hold was quiet, like a tomb. I shivered. Either François and his posse had forgotten about me, or they were deliberately leaving me here to rot.

Maman and Papa had never spoken about my role in my brother's death. But my guilt hung in the air like a thick fog, following me wherever I went. Papa was always so dependable. He would never let my mother down, or any of us. He would do whatever it took to keep us safe, even fleeing the only home any of us have ever known in the dead of night.

I couldn't fail *Maman* again.

Chapter 10

Resolve

Maman! How long had I been confined? Would she be wondering where I was? I struggled to pull my hands free of the ropes. They rubbed painfully against my wrists but would not budge. Maybe if I stood up I could push open the top. There was little room to move in the barrel with my knees under my chin and my hands tied behind my back. I struggled to try to stand but could not get any leverage with my hands tied behind my back. I pressed my back against the barrel and pushed my hands onto the bottom lifting up onto my fingertips. My back and knees pressing hard into the barrel, I could get just enough room to slip my hands under my bottom. I wiggled around trying to slip one foot through my bound hands. I was soon puffing with the effort. The air was warm and stuffy in the barrel. Now for the second foot. Finally, my hands were in front of me. I pressed my lips to a hole in the side of the barrel from which the contents had been removed. The wood smelled of smoky oak and red wine. I sucked in the fresh air in large gulps and then leaned back trying to slow my breathing and the thumping of my heart.

What now? I raised my hands up and pushed against the top. It didn't budge. I gritted my teeth and strained harder. I felt the lid give slightly. There seemed to be a heavy weight resting on top of my prison. My arms were shaking with the strain. Finally, I let the top fall back into place with a thunk.

I was going to need more leverage. I wiggled and twisted, trying to untangle my legs and to get them beneath me. Then I stretched up inch by inch until my shoulders were pressed against the top, and my head was bent over with my chin pressing firmly into my chest. I pulled in as much breath as was possible in this position, readying myself for the coming effort. One, two, three!

With the full weight of my body, I was able to lift the weight. The lid rose and then clattered to the deck. I was standing. I looked up to see two small dark eyes, not more than three inches away, staring at me.

"Ahhh!" I involuntarily exclaimed.

I looked into the face of a rather short, stout sailor with a leathered face and full beard, speckled with grey. His piercing stare seemed to see right through me.

"Hmph," he grunted and set down the large crate of tiles he was holding.

"Wha' you doin' here boy?"

"We were playing a game, and … I guess they forgot about me."

The sailor untied my hands and helped me out of the barrel. "Better come with me."

I followed him upstairs and to the back of the ship. We came to the door of a cabin, and the sailor rapped on the door. It opened, and I was once again staring into the captain's stormy eyes.

"You again?" he said, raising an eyebrow quizzically. He showed us into his quarters and gestured to the chairs at the large table, which was still covered in maps and charts.

"Found this one tied in a barrel under the stairs. Don' know how long he'd been there. He won' rat on those tha' put 'im there."

"Thank you, seaman. You are dismissed."

The seaman nodded and left.

"You seem to always be in the wrong place at the wrong time," Captain Carteret said. "Who tied you up?"

"We were playing a game."

"So you say. Give me the names of the boys who tied you up."

I hesitated. If I gave their names, what punishment would they receive? And what would they do to me then?

"It is all right. You can tell me."

My throat felt dry. I took a deep breath and shook my head. "They didn't mean anything by it."

"Didn't they?"

I watched the captain pace up and down the length of the cabin, his hands clutched behind him. He stopped and stared out the small window. Then I noticed a small, framed painting sitting on the table. I picked it up and stared into the face of a boy, maybe my age. He had blue eyes and dark wavy hair. His large ears stuck out from his head comically. His large eyes looked sad and his long nose gave him a gaunt, sickly look. Behind him stood a younger Captain Carteret with gloved hand resting gently on the boy's shoulder.

"Who's this?"

The captain turned, crossed the room quickly, snatching the frame from me.

"Your name is Etienne, *oui*?"

I nodded.

"You seem to always wind up in trouble of one kind or another."

"I'm sorry." I said, feeling miserable. Then I thought of the boy in the portrait. I wondered who he was. I knew I didn't want to be a stove-maker merchant, like Papa. And I don't want to be a *prolé* anymore either. And now I could never be a musketeer. But maybe I could be a sailor. "When we were leaving La Rochelle, you called me your cabin boy. What does one do?"

"A cabin boy is about your age and is training to become an officer on the ship. He must learn to tie sailors' knots, recognize different types of ships, read a compass and a map, all so that someday, you can run a ship and command men."

"How could I ... I mean, I don't know anything about ships. But, how could I become a cabin boy?"

"You just need a sponsor, a captain willing to take you on and permission from your father, of course."

"Would you be willing to take me on?" I grimaced, as I heard my voice squeaking like a frightened mouse.

I watched the captain walk to the window and stare out. I could hear my heart thumping and wondered if the captain could hear it too. Finally, he looked down at the portrait still in his hand. He sighed and slowly walked back to me.

"Do you know how to play chess?"

"*Oui*. My father taught me."

After a pause, the Captain said, "I'll make you a bargain. I'll take you on, but just for this voyage. You will serve as my trainee, study mathematics, navigation, and run errands for me. Then if it works out, I will talk to your father about taking you on fulltime. In exchange, you will play chess with me in the evenings. My brother used to play with me, and I miss the diversion. Agreed?"

The question sounded more like a command, than a request. I took his outstretched hand. "Agreed."

Chapter 11

Lessons

The next morning, I was eager to start my first lesson. Captain Carteret sat me down at the table and spread several maps out in front of me.

"Do you know what these maps show?" the captain asked.

I looked closely at the first map. Various shapes were drawn along the right side of the page leaving the left side nearly barren. As I looked at the forms, I caught a word I recognized and squinted closer at the fine print, La Rochelle. A faint line had been drawn a little way out from it with small points plotted at various places along it. I smiled. "It's a map showing the land of Europe and the blank space is the sea."

"Very good, Etienne. This is La Rochelle," he said, pointing at the fine print, "where we began this voyage. What do you think this line coming out from it represents?"

"That must be our path."

"It is. Now why do you think I need to track our path?"

"So that we know how much further we have to go?"

"Yes. Why else?"

I thought about it. "I guess it's important to know where we are and where we are going so that we don't get lost."

"Good. Now look at these markings on the map. I know they are hard to see. What do you think they represent?"

Some of the markings looked like rocks, others like the patterns the waves made when they smashed into the harbor walls. "Are those obstacles we need to avoid?"

"They are, good. Now how do we determine our progress?"

I shrugged.

"If we know how fast we are going and the direction we are heading, we can calculate the distance we have traveled. Then we have to convert it to the scale of the map. To do that, we have to determine our latitude, which is represented by these lines."

"So, these points you have marked represent when you have calculated the ship's actual location?"

"Yes, excellent! I have had many cabin boys who took far longer than this to catch on to these basic concepts."

"Was the boy in the portrait with you a cabin boy?"

"He was."

"Where is he now?"

Captain Carteret frowned and pressed his lips together.

"I'm sorry. I shouldn't have asked." I said, quickly.

The captain sighed. "He was my sister's third son. My brother-in-law asked me to take him on and train him to sail. It was against my sister's wishes, but the boy's father insisted, so I agreed. He was a quick study, too, and loved the sea."

"What happened?"

Captain Carteret paused. "That is all you need know for now. Look back to your maps."

As the morning progressed, the captain turned me over to his first mate, who took out a round brass device he called a compass.

"This is the first step in learning to calculate the ship's position on a map. Start by learning the four main directions: north, south, east and west. Then you'll learn the directions in between." I spent the afternoon pouring over the map and compass. The time passed quickly and before long, the captain returned from his turn on deck.

"Let's begin again tomorrow morning," Captain Carteret said. "In the meantime, take this book and study the ship sketches so that you can learn to recognized them."

"*Oui.* Thank you," I said and hurried out to find a quiet place to study.

The next morning, I was back at the captain's quarters ready to learn more.

"Today I want to teach you how to tie a seaman's knot, called a bowline," Captain Carteret said, taking two lengths of rope and tossing one to me. "Form a loop at the end of the rope. Then pass the end of the rope through the loop, like this … then around the standing end and back through the loop."

He demonstrated how to tie the knot slowly.

I looked dubiously at the length of rope.

"Take the rope and make a loop, like this," the captain said, waiting for me to copy what he did. "Now take the other end, call it the rabbit. The rabbit comes out of the hole …"

He paused waiting for me to catch up.

"… then runs around the tree and goes back down the hole." He nodded, watching me. "Now pull it tight. Good. Now let me see you do it alone."

I felt my brows furrow as I concentrated on tying the knot. I thought through the steps … make a loop … up through the hole, around the tree, and back down the hole.

"Keep practicing until you can do it without thinking."

I stared at the knotted rope helplessly. It didn't look at all like the captain's knot. How could I already forget what the captain had just shown me? "What is this knot used for?" I asked tugging at the knot in frustration.

"It is used for many things, like fastening the mooring line to the mooring post. It can also be used to attach two ropes together," Captain Carteret patiently showed me how to tie the knot again. He paused watching me. "It is important that you learn how to tie this knot, quickly and without thinking. It could save your life."

"Save my life?" I repeated, staring at Captain Carteret.

The captain was staring at me but was not seeing me. I was sure that he was remembering some other time and place. I waited, afraid to break into his thoughts. I glanced at the portrait of him with his nephew. Had he lost him in a storm? I looked down at the rope again, determined to learn the knot.

"Listen to me and hear me well. If you ever find yourself on the deck when a storm rolls in, find the closest rope and wrap the end around your waist and use this knot to tie yourself in. Do you hear me?"

"*Oui*. I will."

"Good. Keep practicing and come back later tonight, and maybe instead of playing chess, we will start learning to recognize the constellations."

"I will," I promised, standing up.

"And one more thing," the captain said, walking me to the door. He motioned to one of the sailors nearby. "Take the lad, show him the deck and teach him the parts of the rigging."

"Yes, Capt'n," the sailor replied.

I followed him out.

My head was spinning with too many names and instructions by the time I returned to the captain's quarters. For some reason that didn't make any sense to me, the large square sails were called *yards*, and they were attached to a *spar* (or beam) at its *head* and pulled away from the mast at the *head cringles*. The side edges of the sails were called the *leeches*, and the bottom was called the *foot*. Okay, so head and foot at least correlate to top and bottom of the sail, but *leeches*? I couldn't understand how the edges of sails made seamen think of the slimy blood-suckers doctors use to cure people of ill-humors. The *foot* of the sail was attached to the *clews* by ropes called *sheets*. It was all very confusing, like learning to speak a different language. Why didn't they just call things what they were?

When I reached the captain's quarters, he had spread large blue maps with tiny stars drawn in random patterns all over. Faint lines connected some of the stars together.

"These are called star charts," Captain Carteret began. "And see these groupings? They are called constellations. If we connect the stars together with these lines, then they look like various Greek or Roman gods. That will help us to recognize them, and then we can determine where we are, based on our relation to the stars."

I squinted at the map. They still just looked like random lines and points to me.

"This is Orion. He was supposed to be a gigantic, mythical Greek hunter who went to the island of Crete to hunt with Artemis, the goddess of hunting, and her mother, Leto. His zeal for hunting caused him to boast that he would kill every animal on Earth. Gaia, Mother Earth, was so angry that she created a giant scorpion, Scorpio, to kill Orion.

The pair battled, and Scorpio eventually killed Orion. The contest caught the attention of Zeus, King of the gods, who raised

Scorpio to heaven in honor of his victory. Artemis, though, had come to admire Orion, and so she asked Zeus to do the same for him. Zeus finally agreed, so that Orion could serve as a reminder to men to be careful of becoming prideful."

"Where is Scorpio?" I asked looking at the map.

"Here." Captain Carteret pulled out another map and pointed to a chain of stars in the shape of a fishhook. "This is the constellation Scorpius. Scorpio and Orion will never be in the sky together."

"Why not?" I asked, tracing the lines with my finger.

"Every winter, Orion hunts in the night sky, but every summer he flees, as Scorpio wakes up from his hibernation." Captain Carteret stood up and put his hand on my shoulder. "Study these shapes and names. When you think you can recognize them, come up onto the deck, and we'll see how you do."

With that Captain Carteret left me alone with the star charts spread out on the table. As I stared at the lines, I saw the great hunter Orion move across his chart of the winter sky and leap onto the chart of the summer sky. I watched as he approached Scorpio cautiously. Scorpio spun to face his old enemy. They circled one another, moving around and around in a great cosmic battle. Who would win this time?

The lamp had burned low, and I was tired, so I left to go find Captain Carteret on the top deck. A great wheel took up the center of the deck. The captain stood off to one side watching the helmsman at the wheel.

"Ah, Etienne. Come here, lad, and show me where Orion is."

I stared up at the sky. It all looked so different without the drawings on the star chart. Finally, I spotted three stars in a line.

"There! There he is. Those three lines form his belt and those two stars are his shoulders. The curved stars are his bow. And that bright star below his belt, that is Sirius, his hunting dog!" I said.

"*Bien*! You are right."

Together we worked our way around the sky pointing out various constellations, while Captain Carteret shared stories about the various mythical representations.

After a time, I sighed. I wished I could share what I was learning with someone. I imagined Nicolas laughing as I retold the stories. Then he would show me what he had learned in his fencing lessons. After I thought of Louis. He, especially, would have loved the story of Orion and Scorpio. I could almost see him reenacting the story enthusiastically as I narrated. I swallowed hard.

I felt a hand on my shoulder and looked up to see Captain Carteret's stormy eyes watching me. We stood there in silence listening to the waves crashing against the hull.

"Whom did you leave behind in La Rochelle?"

"My cousin, Nicolas, and," I paused, blinking back the tears that threatened to erupt, "my little brother, Louis, too, but he ... he died four years ago."

Captain Carteret studied me, silently. Finally, he asked, "Were you close to your cousin?"

"He was my best friend," I paused, "my only friend."

"I see. So those boys did not just forget about you in a friendly game? Hmm? I thought not."

"Nicolas and I were going to train together, to become musketeers. I didn't even get to say good-bye." I fell silent. If I said more, I was afraid he would hear the tremble in my voice.

"My nephew, Andre, the boy in the portrait you found in my cabin," the captain paused and stared out over the water. "He was about your age when I took him aboard. He too always seemed to have a way of finding trouble. Often, he would unknowingly end up in the middle of a fight between two other seamen. In trying to ease tensions, he would become the target. It would often end with Andre scrubbing the decks alongside the other two seamen."

It was a long moment before he spoke again. "One day Andre

stumbled into greater trouble. The cook had noticed that the cheese and rum rations were decreasing too rapidly, and he came to tell me about it. I suggested that he set a guard on the pantry or lay a trap to catch the culprit.

"As to be expected, Andre came upon the thief one night. He told me that he couldn't sleep and had gone to watch the stars. As he passed the pantry, he heard a scraping sound and went to investigate. The door was cracked open, and he saw a seaman stuffing a bit of cheese into his pockets. Andre pushed open the door to accost him and sprung the trap the cook had laid, sending a bowl of flour onto his head. The seaman fled, and Andre was caught.

"I was awoken when the cook dragged my nephew into my quarters by his ear, all covered in flour, demanding justice. There had been no proof that anyone else had been there, except Andre's word for it, and the fact that we found no cheese on his person. But the cook insisted that he had eaten it. I couldn't see how he would have had time, after springing the trap, but the cook would not be consoled, and Andre would not give up the name of the seaman. Since Andre was in this predicament because he couldn't sleep, I determined that he should keep the third watch."

Captain Carteret stared out into the distance. The water looked eerily peaceful in the moonlight, soothing almost, as the silver light glinted off the ripples.

After a time, the captain spoke again so softly I could barely hear him. "Some time after Andre had taken over the watch, a storm blew in suddenly. Andre was swept overboard in it." Captain Carteret paused, but I had heard the tremble in his voice. The Captain was so confident, so sure of himself. I wondered how anything could affect him in such a manner.

After a time, the Captain continued with his story. "We threw a rope to Andre, but he could not reach it. The wind and waves were too rough to lower a rowboat. There was nothing I could do but watch as he drifted further and further away. I spent two days searching for him after the storm abated, but he was gone."

We stood in silence for a long time, just staring out at the stars.

"My sister has not spoken to me since then. She blames me for his death, and she is right to do so. He was my responsibility."

"But it wasn't really your fault," I said. "You couldn't predict the storm would come up so suddenly. And you couldn't have prevented the waves from taking him."

"I should have been able to predict the storm. The signs were there. And I should have trained him better …"

"But if Andre had told you the truth he wouldn't have been there in the first place."

Captain Carteret's eyes met mine and I flinched as if he had struck me. "Is there something you would like to tell me?"

He was waiting for me to tell him the truth about François and the other boys. I looked out at the sea and took a deep breath. "Jean Guenon, Jacques Cousseau, and Paul Philippe Richelieu, invited me to play a game with them." I hesitated. I didn't think Tomas knew what the boys were planning, and he had argued with his bother to free me. "But they tricked me, and François Lefévre showed up. I know he doesn't like me, and I wouldn't have agreed to play if I'd known he was behind it. He told the others to tie me up and put me in the barrel. Then he put the lid on and made sure that I couldn't get out. It took me a while, but I did manage it. And that was when the seaman found me."

"The truth is liberating," the captain said, putting a hand on my shoulder.

I thought of Louis and caught my breath sharply. I had never told anyone what had really happened; that I had disobeyed *Maman*, or that I had left him alone and unsupervised. What would Papa do to me if he knew the truth? I shuddered.

"Thank you for telling me the truth, lad," Captain Carteret said, with a smile. "Now what should we do about François and his friends?"

I sighed. "I don't know… nothing … it's over. I don't want you to do anything."

"There needs to be some punishment. A ship is a community of people living under tight conditions. There is no room for unruliness or insubordination. Had you not been able to get yourself out of that barrel, we might not have found you until we reached Amsterdam. By then, it might well have been too late. No, they must learn that actions have consequences. But that task will fall to me. Now go to bed. I will see you tomorrow, but not too early."

I was tired. I thought again of the conversation I'd just had with Captain Carteret, as I walked back to my family. The captain blamed himself for his nephew's death, just as I blamed myself for Louis's death. But the storm wasn't his fault. It was just bad luck. But Louis ... that had been my fault. I sighed. I missed him. He could be annoying, especially when I had to watch him. But I still missed him. I paused at the rail on the lower deck and stared out over the water. Light glinting off the waves was soothing in a solemn, quiet sort of way. Papa always said that tomorrow would be better. But would it? I didn't think so.

Chapter 12

Geometry

I took the notebook Captain Carteret had given me and walked out into the grey afternoon light. The further north we sailed, the more the sun had hidden behind a persistent blanket of cloud. I longed for the warmth of the sun. As I came out onto the lower deck, I saw François on his hands and knees, scrubbing the deck. I tried to hide a smile, as I passed by, giving him a wide berth.

"I'll get you for this, *prolé!*" he said, as I passed.

I found a corner by the stairs leading up to the bow of the ship and sat down to study. I opened my notebook. In it, I had carefully copied down notes of everything the captain had taught me. I had drawings of the types of ships, sketches of the constellations with notes of where they could be found. I also had ship terms and their meanings, along with a drawing of a compass rose. I was supposed to be practicing the Euclidean geometry sailors used in navigating. Earlier that morning, the captain had assigned me several calculations, but every time I attempted it the answer came out differently. I was tired and frustrated. I had come outside to study the ship designs and clear my head. As I flipped through the pages of ship drawings, I studied the number of masts, and the shape of the hulls. In the margins, I had drawn the flags of France, Spain, Portugal, Great Britain, and Holland. A chill wind blew in. I shivered and turned back to the geometry. I stared at the lines trying to make sense of them.

Then a shadow crossed the page. I looked up to see François and his posse staring down at me.

"What are you doing, *prolé*?" François asked, sneering.

"None of your concern!"

"Everything you do concerns me!" he said, savagely. He snatched my notebook before I could stop him.

"Give it back!"

But François just turned away and laughed. He flipped through the pages examining the rectangles and calculations I had drawn there.

"This looks like some sort of mathematics," he said, curling his upper lip in ridicule. "You were never good at computations. What makes you think you can do them now?"

I reached for my notebook, but he snatched it away again. I watched as he tore out a page of my notebook and let the wind take it into the air. I glimpsed the triangle Captain Carteret had drawn for me tumbling over and over as it drifted out to sea, diving and swerving on the wind.

"Hear that boys, Etienne thinks he can do geometry!"

"Etienne can't even subtract," Jean put in, laughing.

"And he certainly can't multiply or divide," Paul Philippe added. "He couldn't even calculate the tithe needed in our last lesson in La Rochelle!"

The boys laughed.

"What are you trying to be *prolé*? Do you really think you will ever be anything but a useless, dirty, *prolé*?"

François continued to slowly flip through the pages, studying each of them briefly. "Etienne thinks he can become a captain someday! What do you think of that?"

Jean, Jacques, and Paul Philippe all started laughing again, as if he had suggested that I could become king of France. My head began to swim. I felt dizzy.

"Ship masters are honorable and skilled. They are leaders and command respect. You are none of these things, Etienne. You are a useless *prolé*, a manual laborer, like your father! If I remember rightly, you couldn't even keep an eye on your brother for a few moments. How could anyone trust you to keep watch over an entire ship and her crew? You will always be a useless *prolé*!"

I could feel the tears welling up behind my eyes and fought for control.

"What? Are you going to cry? Go ahead and cry baby *prolé*! Cry!"

The other boys joined in with the taunting and laughing as I struggled to control my tumultuous emotions. My head was whirling, and I clenched my hands at my sides. I thought of Captain Carteret and how confidently he stood on the deck observing his men. No one ever questioned his orders or objected to his assignments. He knew everything there was to know about his ship, the skills of navigation, the heavens and the sea. His men respected him. I don't know why I thought I could ever become a seaman.

My hand slid into my pocket and closed around the small wooden figure. I thought of Nicolas again and the musketeers. They were so graceful in their swordplay, and so confident in their demeanor. I thought of the years of training they'd had and the grand adventures. People listened to them, merchants, noblemen, and peasants alike. They were the king's most trusted elite military guard. I would never be anything but a stove-maker, like my father. I turned away from the laughing and jibing of François and his friends. I wished that it had been me that died, instead of Louis.

"François, Papa is calling for us. We have to go," Tomas said, appearing seemingly from nowhere and tugging on his sleeve.

"I'm coming." He dropped my notebook onto the deck and followed his brother toward the hatch amid ship.

Jean kicked the notebook and it skittered past me. Then he and the other boys followed François to the ladder leading below deck. I stooped down and picked up my notebook. I flipped through it and tore out the pages with my crude computations, crumpling them up and flinging them overboard. I watched as they hit the water and bobbed along slowly opening and expanding as they drifted further from the ship. Then I stuffed it under my arm and, stared out over the water, sighing. François was right; all I would ever be is a stove-maker, like my father.

"Better hurry, boy! You're late and the captain's quite put out."

The first mate sounded angry, but I caught the twitch of his eye. Still, I didn't want to keep the captain waiting. I was out of breath when I reached the captain's quarters and nervously knocked on the door.

"Where have you been, Etienne? I expected you two hours ago."

"I'm sorry, Captain."

"Well, now that you are here, let me see how your geometry is fairing. Hand me your notebook."

"Captain, I ..." I started to tell him what I'd done, but hesitated. What good would it do anyway? And the truth was plainly evident; I can't do geometry. Reluctantly, I handed it over.

He turned the pages to where the geometry lesson should have been and ran a finger along the torn remnants of the missing pages. Then he looked me in the eyes, his grey eyes darkening. "What happened here?"

"I don't know. I kept getting different answers. It's ... the math is too hard! ... I can't do it!" I thought again of the humiliation I suffered every time my teacher required me to solve a calculation for the class. I was so slow, usually François, Paul Philippe, or Jacques would start yelling out the answer before I could finish solving it. It made me feel stupid, just like these problems did now.

"Is it not enough that you gave your word that you would learn them?"

I hesitated. "Maybe ... yes."

"Come in and sit down." It was spoken graciously, but it was not a request.

I sat down and stared at the maps and star charts spread out on the table before me. I could feel his eyes boring into me.

Captain Carteret's stormy eyes darkened. "Didn't you sit there four days ago and promise me that you would study diligently and obey my every command?"

"*Oui.*"

"I thought you were a man of your word. Was I wrong?"

"*Non*, but ..."

"There are no exceptions. Either you are a man of integrity, or you aren't. If a man doesn't stand by his word, then he isn't really a man."

"It's just so hard!" I said angrily. "My calculations don't come out right. It's impossible."

After a pause the captain continued, his tone softening, "Come with me."

I followed Captain Carteret up to the top deck.

"Now tell me, Etienne, in which direction is the land?"

I looked over the railing, but all I could see was grey skies and water slapping against the hull of the ship. I turned around in a slow deliberate circle, but the scene was the same no matter which way I looked. Fog pressed in on me, suffocating. There was no horizon. No land. No sun, moon or stars. There was nothing beyond the bow of the ship. There was nothing to tell me where we were. Nothing to tell me where we were going. Nothing at all.

What if there were pirates waiting to board us? We would never see them coming. I shivered trying to rub some warmth back into my arms. I took a deep breath to slow my breathing. I must think. I had never been in fog so thick. I'd seen fog before in La Rochelle, but it was not like this. The fog I knew hovered near the ground or the top of the water in the harbor, usually in the cool hours of the dawn or late evening and was gone long before midday. And I could still see through it, but this fog was like being smothered in a thick grey blanket. I felt nervous and vulnerable as I struggled to think. Yesterday, the land had been on the starboard side, but could I rely on that still being true? I lifted my hand out in front of me, and it faded into the grey. I shivered again.

The wind picked up. Then, the rain fell in a torrent of icy needles, and I was spared an answer. We returned to the captain's quarters.

"I couldn't see any land, but I couldn't see the stars or the sun either. How can you navigate in that?"

"To determine our location, first we will need two things: our current heading and speed. Our bearing, or the angle we are traveling from true North, gives us our heading. See here on the map; this is the last point where we took the latitudinal readings. We know that this is north." Captain Carteret used a ruler and drew a faint graphite line on the map north from the point of the last heading reading.

He continued, "Next, we use our heading to determine the direction we are going." He took a quadrant, a tool that had a flat edge on one long end and an arch above it. He marked the proper angle, and then used the ruler to draw another light line out from the last heading point.

"Lastly, we will need to know the distance we have traveled, as measured by our speed in knots. As the log line is dropped over the side of the ship, the seamen count the number of knots that roll past them during one turn of the hourglass. This gives us the speed. From this we can calculate our distance. If we are traveling 15 knots in an hour, then we can say that we are traveling 15 nautical miles in an hour. If we know that two hours have passed since our last reading, then how far have we traveled?"

"That would be 30 nautical miles," I replied.

"That's correct," the captain said, picking up a caliber, a tool that looked like a large V, and measuring off the distance along the second line he had drawn.

"So, we should be here," he continued marking a small X on the map. "The problem is that there is wind and tide that causes us to drift off of this course. By taking the headings, we can then determine where we actually end up. By determining the distance that we are off, we can account for the amount of drift."

"But it is such a small distance. Why does it matter?" I asked.

"It looks small at first but look what happens as the ship moves further down this course. If we thought we were here," he pointed at a spot on the map south of the British Isles, "when we were actually here," he moved his finger to the east, "we might well land on the rocks off the tip of Brittany."

"So that is why we have to be careful with our calculations," I said almost under my breath.

The captain nodded. "In fact, it is so important that we use triangles and Pythagoras's Theorem to double-check our work. If we know two sides of the triangle, we can determine the third side by using the formula $a^2+b^2=c^2$. Then you find the square root of the solution to find the length of the third side. When the weather clears, we'll recheck the headings at high noon and compare the readings to the first reading and confirm actual location is where we calculated it to be."

"Why does it have to be noon?"

"The sun must be at the highest point in the sky when we measure the distance from the sun to the horizon to determine our latitude, so that our calculations are consistent."

I pulled my chair up to the table and opened my notebook to copy down the Pythagorean Theorem and the diagrams I would need to calculate our latitude.

I studied the captain's examples, and, then, he gave me some data from a previous voyage so that I could practice. I compared my answer to his, and it didn't match. Patiently, the captain walked me through the steps again, until I found my mistake. He gave me several other problems to solve and bid me to keep at it until I could come to the right solution on my own. Finally, after what seemed an eternity, I compared my result to his, and it matched! He gave me one more problem to do, and I was able to complete that one correctly on the first try.

"Good job!" The captain smiled and rose. "I have an errand for you."

"*Oui?*" I said, standing.

"Go and fetch you father. Bring him to me here."

My father? Why did the captain want to speak with Papa? Was he going to offer me a position as a fulltime cabin boy, or would he tell my father that I learned too slowly and was a waste of his time?

"Quickly now."

I hurried off.

Chapter 13

Proposals

I found Papa on his mattress below the cargo hold trying to read the Bible by the light of a small lantern hanging above him. He had hardly left his mat for the whole of the trip. Maman was on the next mattress singing softly to Lidie and the baby. Neither of them had eaten much since boarding the ship. What little they did eat seldom stayed down for long.

"Papa, Captain Carteret wants to speak with you."

"Why me?"

"I don't know, but he told me to fetch you."

"I am not presentable."

"Please, Papa!"

"Alright, stand still so I can steady myself. I will be glad when we finally reach solid ground!"

Papa had to walk hunched over with one hand on the rafters above him to keep from knocking his head on the low beams.

"This way, Papa," I said, winding through the maze of hammocks and bedrolls to the ladder. Papa followed unsteadily. I led him up the ladder and then aft, towards the back of the ship, to the stairs leading to the upper deck. When I scrambled out into the chilly air, I took a deep breath and waited for Papa to reach me. Then I ducked under his arm, so he could place his hand on my shoulder to steady himself.

"Wait just a minute," Papa said. "I need a moment to take in the fresh air."

After a moment or two, we moved toward the captain's cabin, and I rapped on the door.

We were nearing Holland and would be docking in Trexel soon. Why did the captain want to speak to Papa? I both hoped and feared that he might ask him to let me stay on as his cabin boy. Mostly, I enjoyed my studies. The calculations were still difficult sometimes. But I was learning to love the sea and the rocking of the ship. The past couple of days had been stormy causing many on board great misery, but not me. It would be exciting to go to sea and part of me hoped the captain would ask Papa to let me stay aboard with him. Still, I was not sure I wanted to leave *Maman* and Papa.

As Captain Carteret opened the door, I was immediately surprised by how tall and broad Papa was in comparison to the captain. Papa had to stoop low to pass through the doorway.

"Welcome, Brother," the captain said, looking Papa in the eyes. Then motioning to a chair, he added, "please sit."

Papa just stared at the floor, nervously wringing his cap in his large hands. So, I took his arm and led him to the chair, motioning for him to sit.

"As you may know, we are nearing Holland and the end of our voyage. So, I wanted to take this opportunity to thank you for the use of your boy. He has been a great help to me."

Papa nodded once in acknowledgement, but kept his eyes lowered, clutching his cap tightly. The silence was uncomfortable. Why won't Papa speak? I was afraid he would offend the captain.

"Did you hear the captain, Papa?" I said, softly. "Our voyage is almost finished. Won't that be nice?"

Papa looked at me, and he looked sad, though I didn't understand why.

"Will you take a drink of rum?" the captain said, pouring two glasses and offering one to Papa.

Papa took it. I noticed that his hand was shaking slightly. He downed it quickly, and the captain refilled his glass.

Finally, Papa found his voice. "Thank you … for what you have done for my family … and for me. I know you have risked your life taking us out of France. I don't know how I can thank you properly … I hope we have not disrupted your business too much."

"Risk has always been a part of my business. But times are changing. I fear the king is going down a path from which France will not recover."

"And …" Papa continued, his eyes on the floor, "thank you for working with my son."

"It has been my great pleasure," the captain said. "He is a quick study."

Papa took another drink.

"Not so quick in calculations," I muttered.

Papa looked at me and, then, slowly, looked up at the captain. "I am happy to see him continuing his studies. It has kept him out of trouble."

"Your son has taken to the sea easily. I would be happy to continue his lessons and take him on as my cabin boy, if you would permit it. He would likely make midshipman within a year or two."

"It would be a great opportunity for him … I do appreciate the offer," Papa said. "I am sorry, I cannot allow it. Etienne is my only son now. He is needed at home to help his mother, and to help me with the workload."

I looked from Papa to the captain and back to Papa. For the first time in my life, I felt like I truly belonged. And now Papa was taking that away from me, just like he took away my opportunity to become a musketeer! I might even have been able to see Nicolas again. My heart was pounding in my ears. I set my jaw and frowned.

"I understand," the captain said, nodding thoughtfully.

I did not want to be a stove-maker merchant! But, there wasn't anything I could do about it now. I took a deep breath and sighed in resignation. I felt as if a huge weight had landed on my shoulders, and I wasn't sure I would be able to bear the weight.

"What do you plan to do when we arrive in Holland? Will you stay? There are many who stay only long enough to book passage to England or the Americas," Captain Carteret asked Papa.

"I don't know as yet. My wife only recently gave birth to my youngest daughter. We would like to have her christened, and my wife needs time to fully recover. After that, I don't know."

"Perhaps you would consider moving to New Netherlands? I could use help with the upkeep of a property I have purchased on Manhattan Island in New Amsterdam. I maintain a house there since I am often transporting goods from there to France and back again. The colony is governed by Pieter Stuyvesant, a stern and disciplined man. But it is well-run, and one can worship as he pleases." The captain looked off into the distance and smiled, almost to himself. "And it never hurts to have options should it become too dangerous to remain in France."

Then turning to me, Captain Carteret continued, "There are many cherry trees on my land. They are quite stunning in the springtime. I will give you a letter of introduction to give to my bookkeeper, who lives in New Amsterdam, a city at the southern tip of the island, where the port resides. He will ensure that you are provided rooms on the property. I will also provide you with a letter to give to whichever captain may bring you over. Perhaps, he will agree to continue your lessons, should you so choose."

"That is quite unnecessary," Papa said.

"Not at all! I will not be dissuaded. Your son may use them or not, as you wish, but at least he will have the option, should you choose to go to the New World." Then looking at me directly, he said, "be sure to stop by here before you disembark, Etienne, and I will give you the letters."

"*Oui*," I said, smiling.

We all stood, and the captain shook Papa's hand. Then he took my hand, and said, "I will miss your company, young man. Good luck to you all."

"Thank you, Captain, for everything." I wanted to say more, but I couldn't. I turned and followed Papa out.

Part 2, Refugees

October 9, 1660

Amsterdam, Netherlands

And it came to pass, when they had brought them forth abroad, that he said, Escape for thy life; look not behind thee, neither stay thou in all the plain; escape to the mountain, lest thou be consumed. — *Genesis 19:17*

Texel Harbor, Netherlands, 17th Century
Return to Amsterdam of the Second Expedition to the East Indies (1599),
by Hendrick Cornelisz Vroom
Rijksmuseum, Amsterdam

Amanda M. Cetas

Chapter 14

Land

I stood on the starboard side of the ship, near the bow staring out over the water as we approached Texel port in the Netherlands. The lower hold had emptied out so that the tired, stinking mass of unfortunate travelers were crowded around me anxious for solid ground and fresh air. The cold breeze cut through my thin jacket, and I shivered in spite of the great press of people.

The mouth of the shallow narrows between the island and mainland was called the *roadstead*. It was guarded by a large diamond-shaped fort surrounded with high, sloping walls and five cannon posts at each point jutting into the vast mote, isolating it from the rest of the mainland. All but a couple of the smaller sails had been pulled in so that the ship moved slowly through the channel. Men in the crows' nests watched for any sandbars that could beach the great vessel.

Many ships of all sizes, many flying Dutch flags with wide hori zontal stripes of red, white and blue filled the harbor. I recognized many of the larger brightly painted ships as merchant ships, great three-mast galleons with square rigging. There were also many warships, defended with three rows of cannon along each side. Several smaller vessels, with single- or double-gaff-sails, and 10-man rowboats shuttled between larger ships and the docks. I was grateful for my studies with Captain Carteret. I enjoyed studying the ships and had spent as much time as possible examining the diagrams and insignia of the dominant merchant vessels and warships. Off to the port side, I saw a large warship with a decorated stern, that told me it belonged to an important captain.

Rows of houses with sharply-pitched roofs lined the shore. I could feel excitement building all around me. I put my hand in my jacket pocket to feel for the notes Captain Carteret had given me earlier this morning. I didn't know whether I would have the opportunity to use them, but it was still comforting to have it. I heard a clatter and splash as the anchor dropped and Papa grabbed my shoulder to steady himself. Lidie slipped her hand into mine.

What would this new place be like?

Slowly, the passengers climbed down the ladders into the rowboats waiting below to take them to the shore. I watched the ships in the harbor, as I waited for our turn to disembark. I was saddened at the thought of leaving the ship. It felt good to be needed or at least wanted. The calculations needed for navigating were difficult, but Captain Carteret was a patient teacher. I had felt like I belonged for the first time in my life. Behind me I could sense my mother's anxiety rising. The crowds were thinning, but still we were held back. Papa began pacing the deck impatiently.

"Will they never let us leave this cursed ship?" *Maman* asked, quietly.

I saw Papa talking to the sailor manning the ladder. He looked angry and became more agitated with each retort. I quickly walked over to Papa. It would not be good to make enemies of Captain Carteret after all he had done for us, for me.

"It will be only be a few moments longer," the sailor was saying. "The captain wanted to accompany your family ashore himself."

"I'm sure he has his reasons, but we can manage on our own. My wife is ready to be done with this ship …"

"Papa," I said, quietly, and put my hand on his arm, but before I could say more the captain appeared seemingly from nowhere.

"It is good to see you again, Brother. Come let us disembark." The captain walked over to *Maman* and extended his hand. "Madam, may I escort you off this ship, with your husband's permission, of course."

Papa nodded, and the captain led *Maman* to the rope ladder. Papa took the baby, as the captain helped *Maman* down to the waiting boat. Two sailors carried the baby and Lidie. Papa went next, and I was last. After we were seated, the sailors began rowing us to shore. Large sea gulls circled overhead, screeching and diving for fish in the crowded harbor.

The captain was explaining to Papa that we would have to transfer onto a smaller gaff-rigged sailing vessel to reach Amsterdam because large sand bars had filled in the harbor making it too dangerous for the larger ships. *Maman* closed her eyes at this, furrows marring her brow.

"I will take you to a friend of mine. He will take you safely to Amsterdam. I shall also give you the name of a reputable inn where you can stay until you find more suitable housing."

"Thank you," Papa said and then lurched for the side of the boat, heaving up what little food he had eaten that morning.

Lidie let out a yelp and clung to my arm as we bounced over a large swell. *Maman* sat stoically with her eyes shut tightly and mouth working what I knew to be the Lord's prayer, over and over again. Fish swarmed over Papa's leavings and gulls in turn swooped down to catch the fish. But, despite my family's discomfort, I was awestruck at the business of the harbor. There was so much to see and hear.

I wondered how the sailors, rowing with their backs to the bow, or the front of the ship, maneuvered so deftly among the larger vessels to finally enter the small bay. The boat barely kissed the weathered, wooden dock before one sailor leapt out of the boat, landing gracefully on the planks, and tied the boat firmly to the moorings. A second seaman followed him in similar fashion. Then two other sailors stood and helped *Maman* to the dock. Lidie and the baby were lifted up and handed over next. Then Papa stepped out unsteadily, grabbing the hand of a burly seaman on the dock. When it was my turn to climb out of the boat, I stood up on the wooden seat preparing to leap onto the dock. The seaman, who had just helped Papa held out a hand for me, but I shook my head. I had easily adapted to the rocking of the ship. I could do this too, without their help. I jumped preparing to land confidently on the dock. But as my foot connected with the deck, I felt it slide out from under me. I swung my arms around trying desperately to correct my balance, only to land hard on my rump a moment later.

Laugher erupted all around me and I looked up to see one sailor slapping his thigh in glee. Lidie was laughing so hard that she was crying. Even Papa was trying to hide his mirth.

Maman rushed forward. "Are you hurt?"

I felt my cheeks burning as I struggled to my feet. I wondered how the sailors before me were able to make such a smooth landing onto the dock, so slick with algae.

"I'm fine!" I muttered, brushing past *Maman*. My ankle throbbed, and I felt a large wet spot on the seat of my pants.

One of the sailors slapped me on the back, chuckling. "That first step is always the hardest!"

I wished I could crawl into a hole and just disappear. Pain shot through my leg, and I nearly went down again, as I tried to make room for the others in the boat to follow. Lidie was still giggling. I took a deep breath and carefully followed Papa along the dock.

Once we were all ashore, the captain led us to another dock and went to speak to the captain of a small sailboat with two masts fitted with gaff sails. Rather than having a large crossbeam hung from the mast, like a cross, the gaff sails had a much smaller beam angling upwards off one side of the mast to hold a somewhat triangular sail. The advantage of this design was that the sail could catch the wind from a wider range of directions without over-balancing the boat and capsizing it. Having never been on one of these smaller sailboats before, I was excited to get started.

"Another boat?" *Maman* said, wearily, looking at Papa. "Can't we just stay here?"

"I'm sorry; no. This is a whaling and fishing town. We need to go to Amsterdam, where there will be more trade work to be done. You will like the city. I am told it is much like La Rochelle," Papa said.

But it wasn't at all like La Rochelle.

Chapter 15

Amsterdam

It took us nearly all afternoon to reach the port at Amsterdam. When we arrived, the sailboat captain said something to the ferryman and indicated we should disembark. *Maman* wanted to walk to the inn, but the captain shook his head and started to load our trunk onto the ferry. It seemed we had no choice, but to climb into the small boat. But *Maman* remained solidly rooted to the ground. Papa urged her to get into the boat, but she just shook her head. Finally, the ferryman shouted something that sounded angry and hailed a man driving a narrow wagon, which was pulled by a single horse.

The ferryman loaded our trunks into the back and then helped *Maman*, the baby, and Lidie into the bed of the wagon where they sat down on one of the trunks. Papa and I walked. It was a struggle to keep up with the wagon. The narrow streets were bustling with dogs, horses and people pushing barrows and shifting crates. The air smelled of salt, fish, and pancakes.

Captain Carteret had told me that the city was divided into sections separated by a wide central canal and three smaller semicircular canals. We followed one of them now, keeping it always to our left just beyond a row of elm trees. On our right side a row of narrow houses with deeply-pitched roofs nestled together. They had ornately trimmed façades broken with large rectangular windows and steep stairways branching off to both the left and right sides of the doorway. Smaller radial canals connected the three larger ones, which were crowded with a great variety of large and small rowboats. The city seemed to contain more water than land.

Our journey was slow going as the driver was forced to weave and turn past other carts, often reigning in the horse to avoid a collision. Once or twice the wagon stopped so suddenly, I ran into the back of it.

I heard Lidie giggling after one such encounter.

We crossed one narrow bridge after another. I wished *Maman* had just agreed to get into the ferry as that route clearly would have been more direct. La Rochelle had a pleasing uniformity to it with its lime-stone façades, gracefully arching entranceways, red-tiled roofs and gargoyles keeping an eye over the pedestrians. This city, with its neatly kept houses, bustling canals and narrow streets, was cold, crowded, and foreign.

The driver finally led us into a large market square and stopped along the quays. He pointed across the large plaza to the sign indicating the Delft Inn. A huge building containing five rows of windows and a large bell tower centered on the roof filled the end of the square. Another huge building that looked like a cathedral, but not like any I had ever seen before, loomed in the distance. A smaller, though equally important-looking building with numerous dormer windows, occupied the center of the square.

Slowly, we wove our way through the plaza. Papa lugged the heavy trunk, while I struggled to carry the smaller one, and keep up with my weakened ankle. *Maman* held the baby close to her, while Lidie clung to her skirt.

Around us crowds of people bartered with street merchants selling all manner of goods. I didn't understand their language. It had a choppy, guttural sound to it, not the musically harmonious sounds of French. Children ran in all directions chasing balls or pushing large hoops with their sticks.

"Children should be disciplined with work or studies, not left to roam the streets," Papa muttered.

"But it looks like so much fun!" Lidie said, clapping her hands.

After nearly tripping over one small girl, in a blue bonnet, chasing her runaway hoop, we finally, reached the inn.

I watched as Papa tried to explain that we needed one room for the five of us. He pointed at us and pantomimed sleeping, as he spoke.

"*Oui*," the innkeeper said, smiling. "This way, please."

I saw Papa's face relax, and he nodded. It was a relief that the innkeeper spoke French. He led us up to our room on the second floor. There was a small shuttered window on the far wall, and the innkeeper went over to open it up. I could see the cathedral tower off in the distance. The room itself was small with only one bed for *Maman* and Papa. The innkeeper promised to bring another mattress for the floor for Lidie and me to share. The room was cold, and the innkeeper moved over to the hearth to start a fire.

"Lydia, we cannot stay in this inn long," Papa said. "I must go inquire about a job and more permanent housing."

"But, Husband, we have only just arrived, and it is getting late in the afternoon. Can't you wait until the morning?"

Papa bent down and kissed *Maman* on the lips. I cringed and stuck my tongue out at Lidie. She giggled.

"I will not be long," Papa said, and left.

We waited until it began to get dark, and still Papa had not returned. As the sky darkened, the cathedral bell chimed seven times. Seeing that we had not gone down for supper, the innkeeper brought up a pot of meat stew, hard bread, and a pitcher of mead. We ate the meal in an uneasy silence. Then, Lidie and I went to bed. I could hear *Maman* weeping softy into her pillow. Papa should have been back by now. We were supposed to be safe in Amsterdam. But were we really? What could have happened to him? Maybe we should have stayed in

La Rochelle after all. I closed my eyes and prayed to God that he would bring Papa back home again..

Chapter 16

The Search

I awoke to my baby sister's crying. I slipped out of bed and went over to the cradle. The baby sucked on her fist, then scrunched up her face, and wailed again. I picked her up and felt that her couche was soaked. So, I found a clean one, and after removing the soiled one, I slipped the clean couche between her legs and pinned it in place. Then I picked her up, bouncing her and patting her bottom.

The baby sucked furiously on her fist, whimpering softly.

"Bring her here, Son. She is hungry."

I handed the baby over to *Maman* and went over to the window. Light filtered in through the shutters, and I cracked them open to peer out at the city below. Lidie was still sleeping, rolled up tightly in the blankets. I heard the baby sucking noisily as *Maman* nursed her. The fire had burned out in the night, leaving only a few embers glowing in the hearth.

"Where's Papa?" I asked, as I added another log to the fire, stoking the embers back to life.

"He's not returned," *Maman* said. "I don't know what could have happened to him."

Maman was pale. As she reached out to grab my hand, I could see that hers was trembling.

"You must go inquire about him. Ask the innkeeper, if he knows where he might have gone."

"Yes, *Maman*." I started to pull away, but she hung onto me.

"Promise me you won't go far," pulling my hand from hers.

I nodded, slipped on my trousers, and moved to the door.

When I reached the bottom of the stairs, I saw a large dining room with rows of wooden tables and benches. Several people were sit-ting at the tables. The innkeeper and his wife carried trays of dark bread, butter, and cheese to the tables. I felt my stomach rumble. I wanted to sit down at one of the tables and eat my fill, but I must find Papa first. I stood awkwardly at the foot of the stairs debating what to do. Seeing me, the innkeeper set down his tray and came over.

"Can you help me?" I asked. My voice squeaked embarrassingly, but I tried to keep a brave face.

The innkeeper paused, "Perhaps, perhaps not."

"My father went out yesterday, but he did not come back. Do you know where he might have gone?"

"There are many taverns in this area he might have visited. He did not tell me his plans."

"He said he wanted to find a job and more permanent housing."

"I see," he said, raising an eyebrow quizzically. "What does he do, your father?"

"He is a stove-maker merchant."

"Then he would be looking for the Kleine. Artisans, manual laborers and members of the minor guilds belong to the Kleine. They live and work in the Jordaan district, on the outskirts, well beyond the three canals that ring this city. It is quite a long walk from here. If your father went in search of them, it could be quite some time before he returns."

The innkeeper saw my unease and asked, "Have you eaten?"

I shook my head.

"Then come with me. You won't be much good to your father, if you pass out from hunger."

The innkeeper led me to the kitchen and cut a slab of dark bread and spread it with a generous portion of butter. He then cut thick slices of cheese; finally, he poured a mug of buttermilk. He served me at the small kitchen table, then instructed a young girl, possibly his daughter, to take a platter of food up to *Maman* and Lidie. The girl nodded and hurried to load up a tray.

When I finished eating the innkeeper handed me a skin of watered-down mead, and slipped a hunk of bread, some cheese and hard salami, wrapped in paper, into a satchel. Then he put a hand on my shoulder and walked me to the door.

I stared down the street at the rows of houses and businesses. Where should I start? What would I tell *Maman*, if I couldn't find him?

"Amsterdam is not like other cities in Europe. It is built on the wealth of trade. In France and England, the noble families of the aristocracy make up the highest social classes and live in grand mansions surrounded by affluence. But here we live more simply. Here money rules, not the landed. It is the wealthy merchant families who inhabit all the fine homes you see here lining the canals. Behind them, are the townhouses of the nobility, who wish to keep a presence in the city. Further inland the Calvinist ministers, lawyers, teachers, company bureaucrats, and members of the affluent guilds, who make up the bourgeoisie, live in their well-kept homes. But the Kleine live on the edge of the city, a long walk from here," the innkeeper said.

I hesitated on the steps.

"Watch out for the rabble, the homeless folk. They will act friendly to get close to you but will take whatever you are carrying. Here," he said, handing me the small satchel. "Keep it close under your arm. I recommend you start making inquiries at the Green Leviathan Tavern. It is down the road towards the docks, that way. Many of the dockworkers frequent that establishment. Maybe your father went there for information."

"Thank you for your help."

"Just be sure you are back here before dusk. There are many dangers on the streets after dark."

I started down the steps and walked across the market square, which was again filled with vendors peddling their large pancakes cooked with cheese or apple toppings, chestnuts, woolen hats and scarves, lacy collars, and salted fish. An old woman grabbed my arm and started talking in a language I couldn't understand. She was poorly dressed, and I remembered the innkeeper's warning. Wrenching my arm back, I hurried away clutching my meager provisions close. I slipped on the wet cobblestones and nearly fell. My heart was pounding. I slowed my pace and followed the row of buildings out of the plaza onto a narrow street. A cold wind rustled the yellowing leaves that were left clinging to the trees along the canal. I studied the signs hanging over the doorways, but I couldn't read them. How would I find the Green Leviathan if I didn't speak Dutch?

I slowed my pace further and started looking for other visual clues. I came to an apothecary, judging from all the small dark bottles in the window, and the herbs hanging from the ceiling. There was a strange smell, both sweet and peppery, coming from the open doorway. I moved on. The next shop was filled with white and blue porcelain dinnerware with delicately detailed scenes of birds, trees and funny little buildings with roofs curling up to the sky. Another shop was filled with a variety of furs from animals of various kinds. Some looked like foxes or minks. Others were animals that I had never seen before. There was one large brown skin, with a bushy tail ringed with black and grey stripes. The next shop sold tobacco. Over the doorway hung a sign showing smoke curling up from a large pipe. There were also bakeries and a confectioner's shop, with its windows filled with all manner of tantalizing sweets.

I was nearly ready to give up, when I saw a sign with a green sea monster hanging from a dark-paneled building a few doors down. It must be the Green Leviathan! I hurried to the dingy building and climbed the steps. Even at this early hour there were several men sitting at various tables filling the room. A long counter ran along the back wall and a short, round man stood behind it laughing with another man sitting on a high stool.

I took a deep breath and walked to the counter.

"*Excusez-moi*, I am looking for my père. Did you see him last night?"

The man behind the counter just stared at me.

"Papa is tall and broad," I said, using my hands to convey my meaning. "His hands are rough …"

The barkeep just looked at me.

"He was looking for work and a place for our family to stay."

I couldn't understand why the barkeep just watched me without speaking.

"He does not speak French." I turned around to see a man with untamed dark hair and mustache sitting at a table in the corner by the fire. He hailed me with his tankard. I looked him up and down. He was dressed in a navy-blue coat with gold embellishments and breeches and a sizable white ruffle at his throat. He wore black boots that reached to his knees, instead of the buckled shoes most men wore. A large brimmed and feathered hat sat on the chair next to him. I couldn't help but wonder who this man was. His looks made a stark contrast to so many of the merchants in the street dressed in their black coats and large square collars with their clean-shaven faces and tall hats. He had an air of confidence and danger about him.

When I didn't respond, the dark man continued, "Who is it that you are trying to find?"

"My Papa went out yesterday looking for work and he never came back. I have come to find out what happened to him."

He then looked at me and smiled. "I was also here last night, and I remember seeing a newcomer, as you described. He may have been your father, but it is hard to be absolutely sure. There are so many new faces in here each day. This man went about the room trying to speak to several men and then he left."

I tried to hide my disappointment. I should have known that it would not be this easy and turned to leave.

"Just a moment more, young man," the dark man continued. "The man also came and spoke to me. He was indeed asking where he might obtain work and lodging for his family. He, also, only spoke French."

"That must be Papa. What did you tell him?"

"I told him where to find the Jordaan district. There he can get in touch with the builder's guilds and find housing."

"Can you show me which way he went?"

"I will, but I had assumed that he would go back to his family and would seek out the Jordaan today, as it was already dark when we spoke," the Dark Man said, leading me to the door.

"Papa never came back. *Maman* is worried, but she has my two sisters to care for, so I came in search of him."

The Dark Man held the door open for me, then followed me outside.

"It can be dangerous after dark. The wealth of Amsterdam has attracted merchants, tradesmen, and sailors, yes, but it has also brought gypsies, pirates, and thieves. The Green Leviathan is at a crossroads. The docks and quarters of the shipbuilders are just a bit further that way along this main road." He pointed behind us in the opposite way from which I had come. "If you go in the other direction, away from the docks, you will come to the market square and the political, economic, and religious center of the city. Now then, if you instead go to the right, you will cross the three circular canals. Between the first and second canal you will pass a grand white building, which houses the West India Company. Keep going and after you cross the last canal, you will come to the Jordaan District. There is an almshouse there on the corner. That is also where you will find the minor guilds. Look at the signs; they will have pictures to tell you what work they do. Your Papa headed off in that direction."

"Thank you for your help, *Monsieur*," I said.

The Dark Man laughed. "You honor me with such a title, but I am not a nobleman; I am naught but a ship's captain." He paused. "Can you read?"

"Yes."

"Here is my card." He offered a small card with the name, Jacob Janssen van den Bergh, West India Company written in a neat hand. "Take it. When you find your father, come seek me out. It may be that I have an employment opportunity for your father after all."

I nodded to him and took the card, stowing it in the inside pocket of my jacket with the letter from Captain Carteret. Then I started out in the direction Papa had gone.

As I walked down the road, I thought about what Janssen said about the dangers after dark. I thought about the man I saw abducted in La Rochelle to serve aboard the ship. Could that be what happened to Papa? Had he been captured by pirates and taken aboard their vessel?

I came to the first bridge. It was barely wide enough to accommodate a horse and wagon. I stood for a moment watching the men loading and unloading the small boats moored along the edge of the canal. I studied their faces and dress. Would pirates be so bold as to come ashore in the daytime, or would they come only after dark?

I began to imagine pirates lurking in the shadows and waiting under the bridges to capture some unwitting soul staggering home after dark. As I watched, I saw a six-man rowboat skimming over the water toward me, heading out to port. The men had rough hairy faces and small squinty eyes. I noticed how they kept to the shady side of the canal. One of them appeared to have a peg leg. They must be pirates!

As they approached the bridge, I saw a large burlap bag tied up in the center of the boat and it was moving! They must have kidnapped someone and were smuggling him out to their boat. I hurried to the other side of the bridge and watched as they drifted out from underneath. Could it be my father? It's unlikely they would have held him in town this long. But if I followed them, maybe they would lead me to Papa. I stepped back from the railing as the back of the boat emerged, but too late. One of the pirates looked up and stared at me with his one good eye. I was spotted.

"Move along, boy!"

A gruff voice behind me made me jump. I turned and a broad ogre of a man carrying two large boxes, one on each shoulder, edged by me nearly knocking me in the head.

I looked back at the boat, but the burlap bag had transformed into a long-coiled rope. And the pirates had become ordinary-looking seamen. I sighed and finished crossing the bridge.

I walked another two blocks and came to the second canal bridge. On my right, I saw a large white building overlooking the canal. It had two rows of windows crowned with a dark gabled roof and two chimneys. A formidable arched doorway dominated the center of the façade.

The sun was now high in the sky, and I felt my stomach rumbling. I crossed the bridge and sat down underneath one of the elm trees along the canal. I looked around, but this part of the street was strangely quiet. There was no one around, so I took out the bread and broke off a piece. I also took a chunk of cheese and ate. As I washed it down with the mead, I saw light glinting off something on the ground near me. I moved over to investigate.

There in the dirt was a small silver locket. It looked like the one Papa always carried in his pocket. Carefully, I brushed it off and opened it up. Inside was a delicately painted portrait of a young woman in a blue dress with a wide white trim encircling her bare shoulders. Her hair fell in ringlets. She looked familiar … *Maman*? The picture must be *Maman*, before she married Papa. The locket proved that Papa came this way, but I felt a great foreboding. What had happened to Papa? Why would his locket be discarded so casually in the dirt?

I sensed that someone was watching me. I looked up and was startled to see an old woman sitting nearby, staring at me intently. Her clothes were torn and threadbare. I was sure that she had not been there a moment ago, and I did not hear her arrive.

The woman motioned for me to come closer. I remembered the warning the innkeeper gave me about avoiding the rabble, but maybe she had seen something. I moved over to her. She pointed to the locket and held out her hand.

"No, you can't have it," I said, holding the locket close.

The woman shook her head, and pointed at the locket, and then at me.

"I don't understand."

She became more and more agitated, gesturing wildly. She was frightening me. I started to back away, but she grabbed my arm. Then she grabbed my hand with the locket.

"No. You can't have it. It belongs to my Papa. He lost it here last night. No! Let go!"

The woman clung to my hand. With her other hand, she tapped my clutched fist and poked my chest firmly.

I nodded, "Yes, it's my Papa's."

She nodded her head vigorously and loosened her grip. She pointed at me and then indicated "short" with one hand and "taller" with another. She said "Papa."

"Yes, my Papa's." I nodded.

She started pantomiming a man walking with two fingers and then grabbed the "finger man" with her other hand. She turned her hand palm up to show him lying on the ground.

"Was he attacked?"

She nodded vigorously.

"Where? Here?" I pointed to the place where I found the locket.

She nodded.

"What did they do with him? Where did they take him?"

She used her free hand to lift the finger man up showing he was carried and pointed into the distance.

"Where? I don't understand."

Suddenly, she grabbed my arm and tried to pull herself up. I tucked the locket into my pocket and helped her to stand. She was so frail and small. She grabbed my elbow and started propelling me down the road. She walked with surprising speed; leaning so far forward I was afraid she would fall over if she should let go of my arm.

The old woman stopped suddenly in front of a plain building with the word *Armenhuis* (Almshouse) written above the door. She pointed at the door and nudged me toward it, nodding. Then she turned to go.

I stopped her and reached into my bag and tear off a hunk of the dark bread and a bit of cheese and handed them to her. "Thank you."

She smiled and took the food. Then she turned to leave. I looked at the building wondering what I would find inside. I looked back at the woman, but she was gone. I had only glanced away for a moment. How could she have simply disappeared when she could barely walk unassisted? I started to go search for her, but then I remembered Papa.

Slowly, I walked up to the door and knocked. My heart was racing again. What would I find? Was Papa hurt, or worse yet — dead?

A heavy-set woman in a simple dress and white cap opened the door.

"I am looking for my Papa," I said.

She shook her head and put up her finger. Then she disappeared into the house, closing the door behind her.

I was left standing alone. Was she coming back? Should I leave? Just when I decided that she was not coming back, the door opened and a bean-pole of a man with wispy grey hair peered out at me.

"Madame Annelies had asked me to determine your business," he said in a soft shaky voice.

"I am looking for my père. I was told that he was attacked by someone and was brought here last night. He had gone out to look for work and housing, but never came back."

The thin man said something to Madame Annelies, and she responded. Then he turned back to me and said, "A man was brought in last night. Follow Madame Annelies, and she will take you to him."

The thin man said something to the madame and let me into the house. The woman motioned to me, turned on her heels, and bustled down the hall. I had to hurry to catch up. At the end of the hallway she entered a room, and I followed. There were rows of camp beds lining two walls. Most were empty, but a few were occupied. The Madame walked between them toward the back wall, stopping at a bed in the corner. She turned and gestured to me to take a look.

I felt my stomach knot up. My feet felt like they had stone weights on them. I felt the urgency to see if Papa was lying there and yet, I also felt a terrible dread of what I would find. I reached the side of the bed. His face was turned toward the wall. His breath was shallow and rhythmic. I stood there not knowing what to do.

Madame Annelies walked to a basin and wrung out a damp cloth. She removed the old one and placed the new one on his forehead. He moaned and rolled his head to face me. His eyes were swollen shut and his face was splotched in bluish bruises but there was no doubt — it was Papa.

Chapter 17

Papa

I sat on the edge of Papa's bed and took his hand in mine. His calloused hands — normally so strong and sure — felt weak and frail. Madame Annelies left the room and returned with another poultice to put on Papa's injuries. Slowly, Papa opened his eyes. They looked like tiny raisins set in a puffy purple soufflé.

"*Garçon*, what are you doing here?"

"I came to find you. You didn't come back last night, and *Maman* is worried."

"How did you find me?"

I told Papa of my walk to the Green Leviathan and my discussion with Jacob Janssen van den Bergh. Then I told him about how I found his locket with the picture of *Maman* and of the old woman who brought me here.

"You have my locket?" Papa asked.

"Here it is." I placed it in his hand and watched him open it and look at the portrait. He stroked it with a fat, stubby finger and closed it with a soft snap. Papa brought it to his lips and kissed it. Then he put it away.

"What happened to you, Papa?"

Papa closed his eyes, and, just when I began to think he had gone to sleep, he said, "I started making inquiries in the market square about a stove-maker's or builder's guilds. But had no success. I finally made it down to the Green Leviathan where I also met Janssen van den Bergh. He had never heard of a stove-maker's guild. Apparently, they don't have cooking stoves here, as we do in France. He did tell me where to find the builder's guild and a hospice where we could stay until I can find more permanent housing, but then it seems, I have found it." Papa paused, and I watched a pained expression cross his face. "It was dark when I left the tavern. I was coming here to see if there was room for us when two men attacked me, just after I crossed the second bridge. They took everything. I thought they had taken your mother's locket too. Thank you for finding it." Papa squeezed my hand.

I sat there in the awkward silence, not knowing what to say.

Finally, Papa continued, "I don't know how long I lay where they left me, but I suppose it was some time. It was fully dark, and the cold was setting in. I was in and out of consciousness. I remember someone coming and putting me over his horse. I never saw who it was, though. How long have I been away?"

"You have been gone all night and nearly a day."

Papa furrowed his brows and closed his eyes. It was several moments before he spoke. "I'm sorry, *Garçon*, but I need to ask more of you. You must help me get back to your mother and sisters."

"Of course, I will help you!"

"It's my ribs. I think they are broken. And I have other injuries too, but we can't stay at the inn for much longer. It is too expensive."

"Should I bring *Maman* and Lidie here instead?"

"The robbers stole the money I needed to pay the innkeeper. He won't let them leave without payment."

"Janssen told me he might have a job for you. I am supposed to bring you to him."

"It may be some time before I can work. Tomorrow you must go and see what the job is. In the meantime, I will see what can be negotiated with the Innkeeper. Perhaps there is some way we can work off what we owe him."

I took a deep breath and nodded. "The Innkeeper gave me some food for the noon meal. I ate some of it, but there is a lot left. Take some and eat."

While Papa was eating, Madame Annelies returned to check on him. When he was finished, I tried to help Papa up, but Madame shook her head vigorously and pushed him back down on the pillows. Then she showed me one and then two fingers. She made a fist and moved her arm in an arc like the sun rising and setting.

"He will be able to leave in one or two days?" I asked.

Madam Annelies nodded, showing two fingers.

"Leave me, *Garçon*. Tell your mother that I am mending well and will rejoin her soon. Now get going before it gets dark."

I nodded and hurried back to the inn. The sun was retreating, and dusk was setting in. The shadows were lengthening. I saw an old woman walking hunched over, nearly double. She appeared to be the same woman who helped me find Papa earlier. I ran up to her.

"Thank you for helping me to find Papa."

The woman turned to me, but her features were distorted ending with a long-crooked nose. Her eyes were burning red. She hissed and reached for me with a twisted hand.

I ran. I nearly ran right into two foul-smelling sailors and swerved to avoid them.

"Ahoy, boy! Want a job crewing the pirate ship *Sinjoor*?"

I was out of breath when I got back to the inn. The sun was setting, and the market square was thinning out. I slowly walked up the stairs to our room. I hesitated at the door. How would *Maman* take the news of Papa's injuries and the loss of all of our money? But I couldn't procrastinate any longer. Taking a deep breath, I lifted the latch and entered the room. *Maman* was pacing by the fire. When she saw me, she ran and enveloped me in her arms.

"Oh, Etienne, I was so afraid I had lost you too."

"I found Papa."

"You found him? Truly?" *Maman* pulled away to look at me. "Where is he? What has happened to him?"

"He was attacked by some men. They beat him nearly to death and took all of our money." I let *Maman* absorb this information, before continuing, "A good Samaritan took him to a hospice, where the matron is caring for his injuries."

"I want to see him. Take me to him."

"It's dark, *Maman*. It's too dangerous. We need to wait until tomorrow. Then I will take you."

She nodded and stared off into the distance for a long time. Finally, she said, "We will go downstairs and have a good dinner tonight. Then tomorrow we will have to negotiate with the Innkeeper. Perhaps he has need of a kitchen or stable boy, or a French cook."

"When I was looking for Papa, I met a man who gave me his card. He told me he might have a job for Papa. Maybe he would have one for me?"

"We will decide what to do about that tomorrow. Things will look better in the morning."

Chapter 18

The Dark Man

Lidie groaned when I jabbed her, but then she sat up and rubbed her eyes. I helped her pull her dress over her petticoat and lace it up the back. Then I buckled up her shoes. *Maman* swaddled the baby and we all went downstairs to break our fast. The Innkeeper's daughter brought us food. The room was filled with a variety of travelers, merchants and sailors. When we finished eating, *Maman* went to speak to the Innkeeper about our situation and a possible job. I used the opportunity to go speak with two French sailors smoking pipes by the fire.

"The English have restored their monarchy under the Stuart King Charles II," one of the sailors said. "There are rumors that he is sending a military force to install his nephew, Prince William III of Orange, as the new stadtholder of the Dutch Republic."

"Aye, and there are rumors that war will break out," added the sailor with the red neck scarf.

"Many of the merchant ships are preparing to set sail before Charles's fleet arrives to prevent being commandeered by the English or impressed by the military."

"Do you know if Jacob Janssen van den Bergh is one of those pre-paring to leave?" I asked.

"Might be," the first sailor said. "Haven't heard though."

"Doesn't he sail for the West India Company?" the sailor with the red scarf asked.

"Might be. Haven't heard much tell of him of late. Sort of disappeared, he did."

"Best to check with the West India Company, lad," the red scarfed sailor said.

"Thank you, I will."

Maman returned, so I walked over to talk to her.

"The Innkeeper has agreed to let me help in the kitchen and clean the rooms, until your father is well, but we will still need to pay for the first three nights. Lidie will have to help me with the baby. You will need to find work also. Go see if you can find that merchant who helped you yesterday. See if he will hire you in place of your father."

"Yes, *Maman*, I will."

I decided to go the Green Leviathan first, since that was where I first met Master Janssen. When I arrived, I searched the whole tavern, but Master Janssen was not there. Next, I decided to go to the West India Company. The grand white building had looked impressive when I first saw it, but now it looked more ominous and imposing. When I entered the building, I saw a cluster of men dressed in their black coats and breeches and over-large white, lacy collars talking at one end of the entrance hall. I took a deep breath to steady my nerves and walked over to them.

"*Excusé moi*," I said, "Do you know where I might find Jacob Janssen van den Bergh?"

The men turned, looking me up and down, and I was painfully aware of my shabby clothing. Finally, the taller one spoke, "The man you seek has been dismissed. He no longer works for our company."

"Do you know where I might find him?"

"He should be in prison, or hanged by his neck," the tall man continued. "But that not being the case, I suppose you might try the docks. I have heard rumors that he is looking for men to crew his ship, the *Sinjoor*."

"Thank you," I said and turned to leave.

"What do you want with Jacob Janssen?" the shorter man asked.

"He told me he had a job for my father, who is in need of work."

"Be careful, boy, that you are not impressed into his crew," the shorter man said.

The taller man continued, "Are you sure you want to find Jacob Janssen van den Bergh? There must be other jobs you and your father might do?"

"Thank you for your help, Sir." I said, squaring my shoulders. I knew that I must be the man now, as Papa said. I took a deep breath and went in search of Jacob Janssen van den Bergh. He couldn't really be a pirate, just a ship's captain. There was really nothing to fear.

I found Janssen at the docks ordering men to load crates and barrels onto a small barque to carry to Texel. He looked commanding in his dark blue jacket and shiny black boots. He smiled at me as I approached.

"Did you find your father?"

"*Oui*, Sir. Thank you. That's why I'm here."

"Oh? I expected you would bring your father with you."

"Yes, but he has been injured and cannot work ..."

"I see," Janssen said. He listened as I told him everything that had happened.

Once I started talking, I couldn't seem to stop. Then to my horror, I noticed my checks were wet, and I hurriedly wiped my burning face.

Janssen remained silent, and I risked looking up at the dark man. The silence stretched on. What had I hoped to achieve by coming here?

Just when I started to lose hope, Janssen spoke. "It seems that you have a problem, young man. I believe, however, that I may have a solution, provided you are willing?"

"I can't crew your ship," I said, quickly.

He laughed loud and heartily. "I don't know what you have heard about me, but I do not hijack young boys and take them to sea," he paused, "not unless they have wronged me in some way ..."

He sounded serious, but his eyes smiled, and I relaxed a little bit. "What then do you offer?"

"I will put to sea soon, but I will need some errands run in the next few days. Perhaps you can run them for me?"

I nodded quickly. "I will not let you down."

"We will see. Here is your first errand. You must go back to the Green Leviathan and look for a Scotsman with a braided red beard. He can speak French. Give him this. Then you are to do whatever his tells you."

I nodded and reached for the folded note he offered, but he didn't release it.

"You mustn't tell anyone else what you hear. I do not wish to have my business affairs spread around town. Do you understand?"

"*Oui*, Sir. *Merci*." I took the note and returned to the Green Leviathan.

I had so many questions to think about as I walked, that I didn't see the old woman until she grabbed my arm firmly, making me jump. Instinctively, I clutched my satchel close. Then I recognized the woman, who helped me find Papa earlier. I breathed a sigh of relief.

She tried to pull me back the way I had come.

"What do you want? Let go." I said.

The woman shook her head vigorously and tried to direct me away from my mission.

"I can't go with you. I have a job to do."

But the woman became more agitated and determined to pull me away. I frowned and struggled against her.

She sighed, and grabbed my shirtfront, pulling my face down to hers. She looked into my eyes shaking her head vigorously.

"Please let me go." I said, pulling away from her grasp.

I heard two men arguing behind me and turned to see what was happening. They appeared to be arguing over some document the one man was waving around in the air. I turned back to the old woman to explain why I must go, but she was gone.

I entered the tavern and waited a moment allowing my eyes to adjust to the dim lighting. The room bustled with men of all sorts and serving maidens moving between the tables. The strong musky odor of sweat, tobacco and whisky filled the room. I found the Scotsman with the braided red beard sitting at a table with several other men in the back of the room. A musket lay on the table in front of him and another was tucked into his belt alongside his sword. But he didn't look like the musketeers in La Rochelle. Instead of a white frilled shirt and dramatic feathered hat, he wore a simple black shirt unbuttoned at the neck and a black bandana tied around his head. I watched as he pulled a large knife and started cleaning the dirt from beneath his fingernails.

I took a deep breath and strode over to him and offered him the note, trying not to let my hand shake. "A message from Captain Jacob Janssen van den Bergh."

The man stared at me from narrowed eyes before taking the note. I watched as he broke the seal, opened it, and read the contents. "More recruits are needed," he muttered. I caught a tinge of excitement in his tone and watched a faint smile flick across his face. I shuttered.

"You can write, boy?" he asked, gruffly.

"*Oui.*"

"Then sit here. Write the names of the recruits in this ledger. Understand?"

"*Oui.*"

I watched as he canvased the room, his peg leg thumping across the wooden floor. Stuffing the second musket back into his belt, he sauntered up to a group of men, clapping two on the back as he edged into their circle. After a few moments he moved on to the next grouping. I watched as he ordered up more ale for several tables. As he approached the back of the room where a man was slumped over with his head on the table, he motioned to two of his companions and whispered something to them. A few men approached my table, and I wrote their names in the ship's ledger. That done, I looked up to see Red Beard's associates carrying the unconscious man out of the tavern. As the door opened, I saw that it was getting late. Darkness had settled in, and I worried about how I would safely get back to the inn.

"How did you lose your leg?" I asked when Red Beard returned.

"Fishing accident," he replied.

"It's getting dark. I need to go home now. Please excuse me."

"There's a ferry outside. Get in. I'll take ye home."

An uneasy feeling settled in my gut as I headed for the door. Making a wide detour away from the ferry, I headed for the inn. Before I could get far, Red Beard came up behind me and steered me to the small boat moored in the canal. He lifted me into the bow. I watched in horror as two men exited the tavern, carrying another barely conscious man between them. They lowered him into the ferry, and I noticed the other man already deposited into the hull.

A short, stout man untied the rope, and we drifted out into the canal. Panic rose in my throat. The trees transformed into sea monsters with long necks and mouths of sharp teeth rearing up out the water to snatch me. Where were they taking me? I realized with a sinking feeling that I was in trouble. I needed to get out of this boat, but the way was blocked. I looked for a way to escape, but there was none.

I was trapped …

Chapter 19

In Service

The sea monsters slipped away as a large form took shape in the blackness. Light shown from upper windows of the massive vessel before us. The stars were blocked out by the height and breadth of the ship. The beating of my heart drowned out the grunting of the men rowing and the slapping of the water against our small boat. We drifted closer and closer.

Suddenly, I felt the boat bump into an unseen obstacle. The boat stopped, and Red Beard grabbed my shoulder.

"Time to go, boy," he said, gruffly. He forced me to stand, but we were still too far from the ship. Red Beard picked me up and tossed me overboard. I let out a cry as my legs crumpled onto the hard cobble stones, instead of the expected cold water. I stared into the darkness, and the ship melted into the row of buildings edging the square. I scrambled to regain my feet.

"Now remember, boy, to tell no one of what you've seen tonight. The captain will send word to you at the inn if you are needed again. If you speak of this night, you may well wake to find yourself out to sea as a member of the crew."

So, I was not to be kidnapped after all! I could hear my head thumping loudly in my chest. I watched as Red Beard pushed the boat off into the water.

Over the next three days Captain Janssen sent for me often to deliver instructions to Red Beard or to the first mate supervising the activities at the dock. Sometimes he sent me to various merchants with requisitions for rum, bread, salted fish, sausage, or meade. This morning after breaking our fast, I sat by the fire showing Lidie how to tie simple sailor's knots with a length of rope while *Maman* helped with the cleanup in the kitchen. The baby was sleeping in a basket near us, satisfied from her recent feeding. Most of the other guests had left to go about their daily business, leaving us alone in the dining hall.

"Watch what I do and copy me, Lidie. Make a loop in the end of the rope so it looks like a cross with the short end on top. Take the other end in your right hand … the other hand, Lidie. That's right. Now pretend it's a bunny. The bunny comes up out of his hole, runs around the tree and runs back down the hole."

"It's not working!"

"Okay, try it again."

Suddenly, the front door banged open and Jacob Janssen strode into the dining hall. He looked particularly ominous standing there flanked by two large, nefarious-looking servants. He saw us and acknowledged my wave. Then he turned on his heel as the innkeeper scurried into the room, turning his back to me. I became more uncomfortable as they continued to talk. What could they be saying? Why didn't he come over to talk to me?

Abruptly Janssen turned around and caught me staring at him, my mouth gaping like a fish. Flustered, I turned my attention back to Lidie and tried to explain again how to tie a bowline knot. I watched out of the corner of my eye as Janssen crossed the room toward me.

His servants followed closely.

"I am here for you and your family," he said, when he approached. "Take me to your room so that we can retrieve your belongings."

The commanding tone with which he spoke, alarmed me. "Why? I must find my mother first."

"The innkeeper is getting your mother, as we speak."

"But we owe the innkeeper ..."

"I have made arrangements with the innkeeper, guaranteeing a loan until your father is able to repay it. So, now you will all work for me."

I suddenly felt as if someone was squeezing the air out of my body. What had I gotten my family into now? Papa was relying on me to take care of the family, but instead I had sold them all into indentured servitude. I struggled to think of what to do, but there was nothing coming to me. So, I picked up the baby and led the way to the stairs. Lidie followed on my heels.

"What's happening, Etienne?"

"Not now, Lidie. It'll be okay." And I hoped that it would be, but I wasn't so sure ...

When we reached our room, I quickly packed what few things we had used back into the trunks, and the two brutish men carried them away.

Just then, *Maman* entered the room, "Who are those men, and where are they taking our trunks?"

"*Maman*, this is Jacob Janssen van den Bergh."

"It is a pleasure to make your acquaintance, Madam," Jacob Janssen said. "I would like to employ your husband to build a stove for me, and I was hoping that you would agree to help run my household in my absence."

"But what of our bill? And how will your father find us?"

"Do not fear, Madam. Everything is well in hand. Your husband has already been retrieved and brought to my home."

"I am grateful for your kindness, Sir. I will do as you ask."

An elaborate covered carriage drawn by four horses stood outside the inn. Our trunks had been loaded onto the back. The driver opened the door and *Maman* allowed Jacob Janssen to help her into the cabin. In La Rochelle, I had seen carriages even more elaborate than this one, with intricately carved embellishments and gold trimming. The French nobility used such extravagances to carry them to social engagements, often even employing a second to carry their attendants, but I had never seen the inside of one. To actually ride in one was a luxury be-yond anything I had ever thought possible. My turn came, and I hesitated. I looked down at my clothes and felt ashamed. What if I dirtied the fine red velvet cushions?

Lidie's excitement was evident on her young face. "Hurry, Etienne! Did you see the horses? Aren't they beautiful! I like the one with the white star on its nose best."

I looked across at *Maman*. She looked so comfortable and at ease, like a queen, despite her humble clothing, and I wondered again what life she must have had before marrying Papa. Jacob Janssen van den Bergh gave an order to the drivers and slid in beside me. The carriage jolted forward and settled into an easy rocking motion. *Maman* and Janssen engaged in easy conversation, but I was not listening.

As I watched the narrow row houses drift past the window, I wondered why this dark stranger of obvious means wanted to help us? And why would he pick us up in such luxury if we were to become his servants? It all felt so wrong.

The carriage pulled up to a large row house nearly twice the width of the others on the street and stopped. Janssen escorted us to the door. We were greeted by a slender woman with skin as dark as mahogany wood. The whites of her eyes and her teeth seemed to glow in contrast to her dark eyes and lips. We entered the front room. The floors and ceiling were dark polished wood. One wall was dominated by one of the largest fireplaces I'd ever seen. I could nearly stand in the hearth, and my head would still not touch the mantel. I saw a girl about my age, sitting by the fire working on her stitching.

"Papa!" the girl said, running over and embracing Jacob Janssen.

"This is my daughter, Magdalena."

Magdalena was the most beautiful girl I had ever seen. Her golden hair curled past her shoulders to graze the small of her back, but her shockingly blue eyes looked at me fiercely.

Janssen patiently explained something to her in Dutch.

Magdalena just shook her head and stamped her foot, her arms crossed tightly across her chest. Finally, she curtsied, though a frown remained firmly etched on her face. Then she ran out of the room.

Janssen said something to the dark woman and then turned to us. "I must go see to some arrangements. Chloe will take you to your room." We followed the dark woman toward the back of the house. The kitchen was rather sparsely furnished for the large space, with only a table and chairs, another large fireplace, a narrow counter and a wooden cabinet.

"I don't understand how they can cook on those open fires," Maman sputtered as we passed.

Chloe then led us into a smaller room behind the kitchen. Two short beds framed with curtains were built into cubbies in the walls about three feet off the floor, so that one had to climb up into it. A small wooden cradle occupied the space between the beds. Papa was leaning against the wall in one of the beds.

"Oh, Etienne!" *Maman* said hurrying to him.

Our trunks had been brought in, and we settled into the room quickly. The next morning, Papa got out of bed and hobbled into the kitchen. There he conversed quietly with Janssen. While they were talking two sailors arrived at the back door.

"Well, I'm off to Africa," Janssen announced and handed Papa a bag of coins. He turned and embraced Magdalena, speaking softly in Dutch. She burst into tears and ran off. I didn't see her for the rest of the day.

At supper, Chloe took food upstairs to Magdalena. When she returned, we sat down on the wooden benches at the kitchen table. Chloe filled two wooden bowls with the stew and headed for the back door.

"Chloe, you are welcome to eat with us," *Maman* said.

"Oh, no Ma'am. I couldn't. My boy is waiting for me."

"Bring him down too."

"Oh no, it wouldna be proper."

"How old is your boy?"

"He's younger than your son, but older than your girl."

"Well then, maybe tomorrow you could introduce your son to Etienne."

"Yes, Ma'am, will do. Good night all."

"Good night, Chloe."

The next day, the 17th of October, Papa got us up early. It was still dark outside and quiet. After a breakfast of warm bread and buttermilk, Papa led us to the Protestant church on the edge of the trades guilders neighborhood not far from the Jordaan district. It was still in the pre-dawn when we headed out. *Maman* held the baby and Lidie hung on to her skirts. Papa had a cane in one hand while the other hand rested on my shoulder. It was slow going, but we finally arrived just as the service was ready to begin. During the service, *Maman* and Papa brought the baby forward. The minister then christened her with the name, Mary.

Outside of the church, we ran into François and his family. *Maman* and Papa moved off to speak to the adults leaving Lidie and me with François and his brother Tomas.

"I haven't seen you at Sunday service or Protestant school, *prolé*."

"It's taken us some time to get settled," I said.

"Father's already formed a partnership with the fur-traders guild to fund an expedition to America to purchase beaver pelts. It is a lucrative business. The underfur is combed out to make felt for gentlemen's hats and the pelt will make fine coats for the ladies."

"Has your father found work yet?" Tomas asked.

"We are managing the house for a ship's captain until he returns."

François laughed. "You are servants! I'm sorry for you. I guess we won't be seeing you at school."

"At least we have a nice place to live!" Lidie said, angrily.

"Come on Tomas, let's find someone more important to talk to."

"Maybe we'll see you at Sunday service?" Tomas whispered. He smiled at us and then followed his brother.

When we got back to the Janssen house, Lidie went to find Magdalena, and I went out into the back garden. Since we'd been staying at Janssen's home, Lidie and Magdalena had developed a sort of friendship, even though they couldn't yet speak each other's language. Manicured bushes surrounded two diamond-shaped spaces lying end-to-end between the main house and the carriage house. A statue stood in the center of the first diamond amidst flowering shrubbery. The second diamond was paved with entrances through the bushes at each point in the diamond. Benches were placed along each side and a large elm tree stood in the center.

On one of the benches sat a small boy with close cropped curly black hair. He was so thin and frail. His skin was dark, like chocolate, but not nearly so black as Chloe's. He leaped up as I approached.

"Hello," I greeted him.

He just stared at me. I could see that he was a good head shorter than I, and he looked wary.

"Do you speak French?"

He shook his head and muttered something that sounded Dutch.

"I am Etienne," I said, tapping my chest.

He seemed to relax some, cocking his head to one side. Then tap-ping his own chest, he said, "Po."

"Po," I repeated, and his face cracked into a smile far wider than should be possible on his thin face. He approached me cautiously.

"Etienne," the boy said grasping my hand with surprising strength.

We both smiled.

Then I had an idea. I motioned for him to wait, and I ran to my room, returning with the satchel holding my nine pins. I set them up at one end of the courtyard, and then tossed the leather ball at them, knocking four down. He laughed again and took the ball from me, as I went to reset the pins. His toss was both accurate and forceful, sending all nine pins clattering across the pavement. I looked at Po with a nod of approval, and he grinned, flashing his white teeth at me. We played several more rounds of nine pins and before long we were chasing each other around the garden. Suddenly, Po tackled me, and we were wrestling on the ground laughing.

Then I heard a loud scolding in a language I'd never heard before. Po leapt off of me and hung his head as he followed Chloe to the carriage house. I gathered up the ball and nine pins and returned to the main house.

Maman had made supper. Lidie set five places at the table while Papa sat at one end hunched over his sketching. He looked up periodically squinting intently at an empty wall of the kitchen. I wondered what he was looking at — I couldn't see anything there — but I knew better than to interrupt his concentration. *Maman* sat at the other end of the table and Magdalena sat across from me beside Lidie.

All through dinner, Lidie pointed to an item and said the name for it in French, until Magdalena repeated it correctly. Then Magdalena would say its name in Dutch, and Lidie would repeat it. I tried to join in, but each time I held up an object and offered its name, Magdalena would not even try to repeat it. In fact, she refused to even look at me.

I wished Po could have joined us for dinner too. Chloe had been so angry when she found Po and I playing together. I wondered why. Every time I make a new friend, something always seems to happen. I felt more alone than I had ever been in my life.

I thought again of my cousin, Nicolas, at home, training everyday with his new sword and slowly improving until one day he was inducted as a new musketeer. Why couldn't the Catholics and Protestants learn to accept one another and their beliefs? Why did we have to leave? Papa said it was all about power. Why couldn't the Protestants just obey the king? Was this about power too, or something else? I sighed. I would never see Nicolas again. Now there was no one …

Chapter 20

Work

In the morning Papa went out to the barn, returning with Po, who was leading a horse that had been hitched to a wagon. He looked at me shyly and then to the ground, before running off. Papa climbed into the driver's seat and motioned for me to join him on the bench. I watched the houses slip past as we navigated the narrow streets moving slowly away from the city center.

I recognized the Jordaan district by the small and simple houses. The tree lined canals and cobbled streets gave way to dirt roads cluttered with open air vendors selling eggs, cheese, butter, baskets, wooden utensils and many other wares. Finally, Papa pulled up to a brickyard and told me to stay with the wagon. After examining the piles of bricks, Papa negotiated with the tradesman. Then, two large men started loading the brick into the wagon along with a heavy barrel filled with lime mortar. We headed home.

The work was hard. Papa still couldn't lift heavy things, and so I was left to carry the bricks into the kitchen, mix the mortar, and build the stove as Papa sat in his chair and gave commands. Sometimes, in frustration, he hobbled over to point out my errors and remove portions showing me how to do it correctly. It was slow, careful work. Occasionally, I caught Magdalena watching from around the corner, but she quickly disappeared each time I noticed her. After several days, the sides were completed. Then, after Papa decided the mortar had dried enough, a large slab of stone with two square holes was delivered and set in place on top of the framework.

"Oh, Etienne, it's beautiful!" *Maman* said when I was finished, but it was not me she was praising. "It will be so nice to be able to cook a real meal."

"I just hope Jacob Janssen will like it," Papa replied, "I didn't have the drawings finished before he left." Then turning to me, he said, "We have one more to build."

We? We had one more to build? You mean I had one more to build. But instead I asked, "What other stove do we have to build?"

"I would like to build one for the innkeeper in settlement of our bill."

"But how do you know the innkeeper wants one."

"I don't, but I am hoping to convince him of the benefits. Come, we shall go talk to him."

The potager's stove (stew stove)
Photo by Marcus Flynn; converted to a sketch.

Papa collected his sketches of the Janssen stove and limped toward the back door calling for Po to harness the horse to the wagon. I gathered up our few tools and put them in the back of the wagon with the remaining supplies. Papa's plan to have me build a second stove explained why there were so many bricks and burlap bags still left. It had seemed unlike Papa to miscalculate his materials, after he so meticulously planned out each stove in advance.

We drove to the inn in silence. When we arrived, Papa climbed out of the wagon carefully. I could see that he was still hurting. We waited a few minutes for the innkeeper to finish settling another lodger in his room before he came to see us.

"Bonjour! It is good to see you again. I am glad your son was able to find you."

"Thank you for looking out for my family in my absence," Papa said. "I want to repay you for your kindness and pay my bill by building a stove for you, assuming you do not yet have one."

"I don't need a stove," the innkeeper said.

"Have you ever seen the French stoves? They are much easier to cook upon than over the open hearth. If I may demonstrate …"

The innkeeper's wife came out of the kitchen, wiping her hands on her apron, and said something to her husband in Dutch.

He shook his head, and replied briefly, moving his hand as if to shoo away a fly.

To that the innkeeper's wife pointed a finger at her husband and unleashed a torrent of words that caused the innkeeper to shrink back a step. When the barrage ended, he sighed and nodded. Then, she smiled, and motioned all of us to follow her. She showed Papa an empty space beside the hearth.

We joined the innkeeper at the kitchen table and Papa unrolled the sketch he made for Jacob Janssen's stove. I watched Papa explain how it worked to the innkeeper and his wife. I could see that she was interested from the way she leaned over the drawing and asked questions of Papa. Finally, the innkeeper agreed to have the stove built and then left to attend to his duties. Papa ordered me to unload the wagon and pile the materials neatly by the back door while he settled at the table to make his calculations and draw a new sketch.

It was dark when I finished, and Papa was pacing back and forth muttering under his breath. I was tired, and I ached all over — my arms and legs trembled as I climbed into the wagon, and my back ached terribly as I joined Papa on the bench. It was not fair that Papa made all the promises, but I had to do all the work!

Maman, Lidie, and Magdalena were waiting for us in the kitchen when we arrived at Janssen's house. We sat at the table, and *Maman* served Papa a bowl of steaming fish stew. I closed my eyes for a moment wishing I could just go to bed. The smell of fish, cabbage, and warm bread danced under my nose. My stomach rumbled, reminding me that I had not eaten in hours. I opened my eyes and there stood Magdalena holding out a steaming bowl for me.

The work in the innkeeper's kitchen took several days. Each morning, father and I rose before dawn, ate, gathered our tools and walked the few miles to the inn, arriving just after the breakfast rush.

"Why can't we take the horse and wagon?" I asked.

"It is not ours, and I will not be beholden to Janssen van den Bergh more than I have to be. In any case, the walk is good for us."

There was no use arguing once father had made up his mind. We walked on in silence. Every day my father got stronger and moved easier, and, still, I did all the work.

We took a brief break at midday to eat, and then we were back at it — father gave the orders and I mixed and spread the mortar, lifted and placed the bricks, readjusted them, received a nod of approval, over and over again. We finished at dusk, returning home well after dark. I was tired, but I began to anticipate our arrival home, as Magdalena was always there to silently serve me a hot dinner. Sometimes, I even caught a shy smile.

Chapter 21

Magdalena

We finished the work at the inn and many more besides. Every time we finished one job my father went out to look for more work. And, within a few days, we would be working again. Happily, I was no longer doing all the heavy work alone since Papa had recovered fully from his injuries. When Papa was out on one of his job hunts, I was left at home with *Maman* and the girls. Today was one such day. I sat at the kitchen table. I'd gotten used to working now, and it was strange having nothing to do. Even on Sundays, though we didn't work, there was a routine — we walked to church for the morning service and back again for the evening service. Then, in between, we ate supper, Papa read from the Bible, and *Maman* played music on the harpsichord and sang. Sometimes, I would even be allowed to play nine pins with Po in the garden.

I still missed talking to Nicolas, though. I reached into my pocket and pulled out the carved wooden musketeer, turning it over to look at the crude detailing. I tried to remember every detail of that day. It seemed so long ago …

"What is it?"

Surprised, I look up to see two blue eyes watching me.

"Do you speak French now, Magdalena?"

She watched me a moment. "Magdalena, name of grandmother." Then tapping her chest, she said, "I am Lena."

"*Het plezier is van mij*, the pleasure is mine, Lena." I smiled. I too, had been learning some Dutch.

Lena smiled. "Is a little man?"

"It's a musketeer. They're the king's elite soldiers in France. They fight with swords mostly, but they also have muskets. My cousin, Nicolas, is training to be a musketeer, but I want to be a sailor someday."

Lena just looked at me. "May I see?"

Slowly, I handed over the figurine.

Suddenly, Lena grabbed the musketeer and bolted out the door. I was startled, but only for a moment. Then I was running down the street after her. She had a head start. We ran down one narrow street after another, dodging carts and people carrying baskets and crates. Finally, we came to the marketplace. She was standing on an upturned barrel holding my figurine over her head, laughing.

Autumn had set in, and I wished I had my coat. Even after the run, I felt the chill and shivered.

"Give ... it ... back ..." I said, between breaths.

Lena just laughed.

"Please, give it back."

"Trade."

Trade? Why should I have to trade? It belonged to me. But I could see that she was not going to give in. What could I trade for it? I thrust my hands into my pockets and found two small coins. I held them up, but she shook her head. I looked around. A little way down the street I saw a vendor selling *pannekoeken*, Dutch pancakes. I walked down and handed the woman a coin. She reached into a basket and removed a bundle from a layer of coals. She unwrapped it to reveal a large pancake the size of a large dinner plate. It was topped with baked apple slices. I could smell cinnamon and sugar mixing with the smell of fresh pancakes and baked apples. Quickly, she rolled it up and handed it to me. It was still warm.

Lena had been watching and jumped down from the barrel to meet me. She held out both hands eagerly. With one she took the pannekoek and in the other she offered the musketeer. I took it and stuffed it back into my pocket.

"Come," Lena said, taking my hand. It felt warm.

She led me to the edge of the canal and sat down dangling her legs over the side. I sat down beside her. Then she broke the *pannekoek* in two and offered me half. I took it, and we ate in silence enjoying the sweet goodness. I forgot all about being cold.

One morning *Maman* announced that Papa and I were not to go to work that day.

"Lydia, you know we have to work," Papa protested.

"Not today, it's Christmas! Your job can wait."

"Lydia, you know the Calvinist do not celebrate Christmas. We don't know the day of our Lord's birth. The Papist only named December 25th so that they could hide their celebrations in a pagan celebration."

"I don't care what your John Calvin says. I know that we don't know the actual date, but I grew up celebrating the birth of our Lord. It was a special day the family spent together."

"Every Sunday is a day the family spends together."

"Today we celebrate God's gift of sending his son into this world."

"Easter is far more important. Today is a day like any other, and we will work."

"So you tell me every year, Husband. But I will have my way this day."

Papa sighed and nodded his agreement.

"Son," *Maman* said, looking at me, "Magdalena has asked to go ice skating on the canals, but I don't want her going alone. There is much to do to prepare the dinner, so I don't need Lidie underfoot. I want you to take your sister and Magdalena skating."

"But I don't have any skates."

"I asked Chloe to pick some up for you and Lidie. These are yours, and these are for Lidie."

"I don't know how to skate!"

"I will teach you," Lena said, entering the room with her skates slung over her shoulder. She wore a white fur coat and cap over a blue woolen dress.

Lidie clapped her hands. "It will be so much fun, Etienne! Hurry and get your coat."

Maman had knitted grey woolen mittens, scarves and caps for us to help protect us from the frigid temperatures. But even with the woolen sweater, it was often not enough. The thought of deliberately spending more time outside than necessary, seemed foolish. But before I could protest further, Lidie and Lena were dragging me towards the front door. Others were already skating on the frozen canal.

A group of boys were racing each other up and down, while a group of girls skated leisurely making graceful figure eights. It did look like it could be fun. We sat down on the edge of the canal and put on our skates. I looked at the blades dubiously.

Lena was the first to jump down onto the ice. She helped Lidie down and held her hand tightly as she found her balance. Lena demonstrated the technique, and then helped Lidie take a few tentative strokes. Lidie slipped a couple of times, but then seemed to take right to it. Before long she was giggling and skating around unassisted. I sighed. It couldn't be too hard then.

I dropped down onto the ice. My feet no sooner touched the surface when both feet took off in different directions and I was left sprawling on the ice. I tried to stand and failed. My feet would not stay beneath me. The harder I tried, the worse it got. I could hear people laughing at me. Finally, Lena came to help. I could see that she'd been laughing too! She took my hands, and I pulled myself up. My legs were shaking from the strain of keeping them together.

Just when I'd think I finally had it, one leg would slip out from under me, and I would again go sprawling. Lena would laugh and cover her mouth with her small gloved hand and come to rescue me. After numerous attempts, I finally managed an awkwardly wide stance with my arms stuck out from my body for balance and head forward. I was sure that I looked like the ugly jester in a ballroom full of elegant ladies in billowy ballgowns.

By the time we were finally called home, I was frozen to the bone, bruised, and every muscle ached. It would have been far less effort to have actually gone to work!

The smell of roasted pheasant, spiced apples, and warm bread made my mouth water. Chloe was helping *Maman* set the table when we came into the kitchen.

"Now Chloe, I want you and Po to join us at this table today. And I won't hear any complaints. It's Christmas, the time for family and friends to share in the birth of our Lord together."

"Yes, Ma'am."

Po sat opposite me at the table, next to his mother. *Maman* sat on one end and Papa at the other. I went to sit next to Lidie and Lena slipped onto the bench next to me, instead of taking the space Lidie had saved for her on the other end of the bench. Lidie frowned. I had to move Lidie over more so as to have any space for myself.

Papa led us in prayer. "Our Heavenly Father, thank you for the gift of your son come into the world as the sacrifice for our sins …"

I felt Lena grasp my hand under the table and snuck a glance at her. She was smiling at me.

"… bless this food to the benefit of our bodies. In the name of Christ, Amen."

The meal was delicious, as much for the company as for the food itself. Afterwards, *Maman* went to take a bag down from the shelf.

"Merry Christmas children!" She reached into the bag and pulled out a gingerbread boy for Po and one for me. Then she gave a gingerbread girl to Lidie and one to Lena.

"Oh, Madam!" Lena said. "Where did you get these? The *burgermeister* has outlawed all such images of people."

"Never you mind. I am sure the children will not leave any evidence behind to trouble us." She smiled.

We didn't need any more encouragement than that.

It was the 5th of May, winter had come and gone; spring had arrived, and with it another big event, Magdalena's birthday. Every time I saw her, she had reminded me of its impeding arrival every day for the past three weeks.

Since the days were longer now, Papa and I would take longer breaks at mid-day, and then work later into the evening. I had gone to the market square at the mid-day break to find a present for her. But I didn't know what she'd like. What do girls like? What would Lidie like? Anything soft and pretty. Everywhere I looked I could see tulips. At one end of the square merchants were auctioning off rare striped and frilled breeds to noblemen for exorbitant prices. In other stands, women sold common varieties in cut bouquets or in single potted or unpotted bulbs for more reasonable sums. I walked over to one stand and examined the cut flowers. A cut blossom wouldn't last long. I turned to another stand to look at the potted plants.

"I can buy one?" I said in broken Dutch and held up one of my own fingers and holding out the few coins I had saved.

She nodded.

Which one to buy? I looked for a blue one, to match Lena's eyes, but they didn't have blue. Maybe yellow to match her hair, but it was too bright. Then, I saw a plant with soft pink blossoms. That was the one. I handed over my coins and bought the flower.

Later, after supper, I found Lena sitting on a bench in the garden studying the maps and images in one of her father's books. She looked up as I approached.

"Happy birthday, Lena," I said, offering her the plant.

She smiled and motioned for me to sit down beside her. I watched as she closed her eyes to smell the flower. Then she leaned over and kissed my cheek. She slipped her hand into mine. Her hand was warm and soft. Mine was cold and rough. I tried to pull away, but she hung on tighter. She was smiling at me. I could feel my heart thumping loudly.

Lena set the tulip on the wall by the back door to the main house, and then led me to the garden gate. We walked along the canal nearest our house. The breeze rustled the leaves of the elm trees as we passed. We strolled alongside the water in silence for a long time. The noises of the city were slowing down as the sun finally slipped below the horizon. It still wasn't dark yet, but more like an eerie dusk. I had never known the days in La Rochelle to go on forever as they did here in Amsterdam.

Lena led me up onto the bridge arching over the water. We stopped at the apex, and I looked down at the glassy water. There was Nicolas staring back at me! But it couldn't be. I looked again. It was Nicolas's broad shoulders and commanding stance. I felt Lena's soft hand slip into mine, brushing over the hard-earned callouses, and saw her reflection appear next to Nicolas's in the darkening water. But, of course, it wasn't really Nicolas. I'd not seen myself in a glass since we had fled La Rochelle. I was shocked at how much my appearance had changed.

I felt that I could stand there forever with Lena, listening to the rippling water.

One by one the stars came out, and I wondered what Nicolas was doing now.

"What are you thinking about?"

"Nothing," I said.

Lena just stared at me skeptically.

I smiled and pointed at the sky with my free hand. "See those three stars in a line? That's Orion's Belt. His sword is the line from the last star on the left to the two bright, close stars below it. And see, there are his shoulders and head," I said.

"Who is Orion?"

"In Greek mythology, he was a giant huntsman placed among the stars by Zeus."

"Papa told me those three stars make up Frigg's distaff," Lena said. "It holds the wool she will use for spinning into yarn."

"Who is Frigg?"

"She's the Norse goddess of foreknowledge and wisdom. She is married to Odin, who helped create the world and gave life to the first two people."

"The hunter of the south meets the northern goddess of wisdom!" I said and laughed.

Lena laughed too. She had the most beautiful laugh!

"We should be going home. It's very late. Papa wouldn't want me out after dark," Lena said, taking my hand.

As we approached the house, we saw a man talking to Chloe outside the back door.

"Papa!" Lena said, dropping my hand and running forward.

"Leentje, my beautiful *doch*." I watched as he enfolded her in his arms, swinging her around in a great circle. Lena had the most beautiful laugh …

Jacob Janssen van den Bergh had returned….

Janssen said something to Lena. She looked at me then quickly away. I was not sure, but her father's smile seemed to tighten. I took a deep breath and slowed my pace. Janssen watched me intently as I approached.

"Looks like you have been busy in my absence."

I swallowed. "I was just showing her the constellations. I didn't mean any harm."

Janssen clapped me on the back, a bit hard and directed me into the house.

"I brought you a present, Leentje," Janssen said pointing to a large box on the kitchen table.

Lena ran to the table and opened the lid. She made a funny little noise and pulled out a dress, like many I had seen the noble women wear in France. It was made of vibrant blue silk with a yellow bodice and sleeves all trimmed in white lace and adorned with pink bows.

"I am told it is all the fashion in France." Jacob Janssen said.

"Oh, Papa, it's beautiful!" She gave her father a hug and rushed off clutching the dress to her tightly.

"My daughter is very special to me, Etienne."

"Yes, Sir. I know."

"I would not want her to form any unsuitable … attachments."

"No, Sir," I said, swallowing hard.

"Or for anything unpleasant to happen, to those attachments,"

"I quite agree, Sir."

"It seems your father did manage to build it," Jacob Janssen said, pointing at the new stove.

"I hope you like it. The fire is built inside here." I showed him the opening in the front. "Then the pans are placed over these openings on the top. *Maman* has been teaching Chloe how to use it."

"Your father did nice work."

"Etienne built it," Lena said skipping back into the room. "His father only told him what to do."

"Really?" Janssen said with raised eyebrows. "It seems you will have your father's talent after all."

But I didn't want to be a stove-maker merchant, like Papa! My hand formed a fist around the musketeer in my pocket. Papa may want me to follow him into his trade, but I wanted to be something else. If I couldn't be a musketeer, then perhaps I would become a sailor. And some day he wouldn't be able to stop me.

Chapter 22

Sinjoor

The evening supper was a lively affair. Father had returned, and Lena looked beautiful in her new dress. We ate at the large table in the formal dining room. There were even padded chairs for each of us, instead of a hard-wooden bench. Large windows looked out over the canal. Several portraits were hung on the walls.

"Was anyone baptized this time, Papa?" Lena asked.

"I did not know you were religious," Father said.

Janssen laughed. "I am not. Magdalena is referring to a tradition we Dutch seamen have. There is a dangerous reef, known as the Berlingues. It lies along the Portuguese coast. This reef is extremely dangerous, because it cannot be easily seen at night on account of the high coastline. Each time we pass it successfully, all of those who have never passed these rocks before, are baptized. Anyone baptized must fall three times from the mainyard (main sail) into the water, like a criminal. It is a great honor to fall yet another time for the captain's credit!"

Jacob Janssen laughed again. "The first who drops has a gun fired in his honor and the flag waved. Then, if those on board are agreeable, we will tow him behind the ship."

"What happens if they are too afraid to drop?" I had seen the main sail arm. It was awfully high.

"Anyone not willing to fall," Janssen said looking at me, pointedly, "is bound, according to our laws, to give a shilling, and if he's an officer, he must pay two. All of the proceeds are given into the *bos'n's* hands until we arrive in port. There wine is bought and shared out among the whole ship's company in the *fo'c'sle*."

"What of the passengers? Are they baptized too?" Lidie asked, timidly.

"*Ja*, yes, the passengers too, if any, must be baptized or pay as much as we see fit." Jacob Janssen laughed again, slapping the table with the palm of his hand.

I hoped I would never have to take a Dutch ship. The mainyards were the tallest sails on the ship. A great gull landing atop them, seemed as a tiny sparrow to those below. It was a wonder anyone could jump from such a height and live.

"So, were any baptized, Papa?"

"*Ja*, Leentje. Three were baptized and another four paid for the wine."

After dinner, I went outside into the back garden with my notebook. I sat down on one of the benches near the elm tree in the center of the second diamond-shaped patio. I opened the notebook and began to review all the many things I'd learned with Captain Carteret. It was peaceful out here with the shrubbery muting the noise of the city beyond its high walls. Birds chattered and flitted through the branches searching for a last meal before bedding down for the evening.

I was deep in thought when I was startled by a touch on my shoulder. I looked up to see Lena smiling at me.

"Thank you for the tulip," she said, sitting down next to me. "It's beautiful!"

I smiled back at her.

"Your father said I should stay away from you."

Lena sniffed. "Well, I don't care what he told you. You're my friend."

We sat there in silence for a while listening to the leaves rustling. A door opened, and I heard the sound of boots on the stone landing.

"Leentje, are you out here?"

"*Ja*, Papa. Coming!" Lena stood quickly and kissed me on the cheek, before running back to the house.

It was getting dark; I couldn't see to read anymore. I stood to follow her, and nearly walked into Janssen, who had suddenly appeared in front of me.

"I thought I'd made myself clear earlier."

"Yes, Sir, you did. I had only come out to study," I said, holding up my notebook.

Jacob Janssen van den Burgh stood rigidly, blocking my path, hands on his hips.

"Truly, Sir. Your daughter sought me out. I will keep away from her. I promise."

After a few more moments he stepped aside and let me hurry past. As I reached the steps, I saw *Maman* standing there. She ushered me into the kitchen.

"What was that about, Son?"

"Nothing," I said quietly.

"It sounded like he was angry. What has happened?"

"It was nothing."

Maman stared at me thoughtfully. Finally, she smiled, and hugged me. "Run off to bed now. Your father has a new job. He will want to start early tomorrow."

I nodded and did as she bid.

The next morning the smell of warm porridge lured me into the kitchen where *Maman* was dotting the steaming bowls with a bit of butter.

"Where did you get this *Maman*?" I asked, eagerly. We hadn't had porridge since leaving La Rochelle. I dropped onto the bench remembering our cozy, stone kitchen at home. It was dark with only one small window. I remembered the smell of the garlic and herbs *Maman* hung above the table to dry. *Maman* used them to flavor our soups and stews. And on Easter Sunday, she would cook a pheasant. I closed my eyes remembering how the smell permeated the house and the taste .... The food in Amsterdam was bland. Spices were expensive, because they didn't grow in this colder climate.

"Jacob Janssen brought cracked wheat back with him from his last trip," *Maman* replied, as Papa joined us at the table. The porridge tasted so good. Later, as *Maman* cleaned the dishes and Papa and I were preparing to leave for our current job, Janssen approached.

"Good day, Gayneau. I have need of your boy today, if you would permit me?"

"*Oui*, Sir. Of course, he is yours. We are grateful for your kindness in allowing us to stay in your home."

"Thank you," Jacob Janssen said, motioning toward the back door.

I saw Mama's spine stiffen and a look of fear pass quickly across her face as she stared at the back door.

A sense of uneasiness settled on me too, and I turned to see Red Beard and one of the other seamen from the Green Leviathan leering at me.

"Papa, you need my help with lifting the heavy stones. I'm sure Captain Janssen will understand."

"I can manage, Etienne. Go with the captain."

I looked at *Maman*, my eyes pleading with her to say something … anything.

She looked the men up and down and took a shuddering breath. Her eyes caught mine, and I could see her unease. She sighed and looked away helplessly.

"Etienne, please accompany my trusted assistants. They will explain the job to you on the way."

Red Beard led me out, and his assistant fell in behind me. What was the job Janssen had planned for me? I thought of the old woman. She had tried to warn me, but I had not listened.

Red Beard directed me through the garden, past the carriage house towards the back gate. I caught a glimpse of the whites of Po's eyes peeking out at us through the doorway as we passed. As the gate closed behind us, Red Beard gripped the back of my neck firmly and propelled me down the street.

"I hear you made a conquest," Red Beard said.

"I don't know who you mean," I stated flatly.

Red Beard smiled, wryly. "Don't be so modest. You seem to have made quiet an impression on the little lass."

"We are friends."

"Friends, is it?"

"What job does Captain Janssen what me to do?" I asked.

"The capt'n did not tell me. You must have patience, boy. We'll get there soon enough."

We walked past the Green Leviathan and rounded the corner in the direction of the docks.

"Is the captain preparing to sail again soon?"

"Aye. Must take advantage of the fair weather. And it does seem that the captain is in need of a good cabin boy." Red Beard clamped a hand on the back of my neck and propelled me toward the docks.

I had to get away. But how? I felt confident that I could outrun this man and his peg leg. But what of the other man? Red Beard had a firm grip on my neck. If we reached the docks, there would be other sailors there to help him. If I was going to break away, it had to be now. If I tried to pull away, Red Beard would just squeeze tighter. And my neck already hurt where he was holding me. How could I break his grip? It had to be unexpected. I remembered the time François's pose tripped me after school. It might work. I could see the docks in the distance. It had to be now.

I took a breath and dropped to my hands and knees breaking his grip. I managed to trip up the other man causing him to lose his balance in the process. Then, I spun around on one heel and scrambled underneath his arm. I pushed off the ground and was up and running before Red Beard could shout. One quick look behind me told me I didn't have much time. I ran like I had never run before. I strained my ears, listening for the sounds of footfalls behind me. I didn't dare to look back again. My heart was pounding. Then, I chanced a glance back as I rounded the corner. I didn't see Red Beard or the other man. I allowed a smile to form and relaxed my stride just a little.

Suddenly, I ran into two men who appeared out of nowhere. They each grabbed one of my arms and spun me around. One bound my arms behind my back while the other bound my legs. Red Beard rounded the corner and looked at me through narrowed eyes.

"Gag 'im!"

I opened my mouth to protest, just as a bandana was thrust roughly into my mouth and tied tightly behind my head. I struggled as they lifted me off the ground, causing them to nearly drop me, but it was not enough. I knew where they were taking me.

"Keep it up, and I'll knock you unconscious!" Red Beard bellowed.

The smell of salt water and fish hit me first, and I remembered La Rochelle. I remembered watching the corsairs carrying unconscious drunkards out of the taverns to the waiting rowboats. I could imagine how scared and disoriented they would be to wake up the next day to discover that they were now part of the crew of a pirate ship. I would soon be one of them unless I could find a way out. I watched with growing anxiety as sails came into view. Then the click clack of Red Beard's peg leg on the cobblestones gave way to a deeper thunk, thunk, as we reached the wooden pier. I twisted around to catch a better view of the ship only to be punched in the side.

"Hold still ye!"

The ship was a barque with two square-rigged masts and a third, lateen-rigged mast. This type of ship was popular with pirates. I knew because it was fast and maneuverable. My heart was pounding, and I felt sure Red Beard could hear it too.

I felt the sway of the tide as the men carried me up the gangplank. What was I going to do? I had to escape somehow, but there seemed no way. I struggled again, and, again, received a sharp blow to the gut. This time I had to gasp for breath. We reached a small storeroom, and the men dumped me roughly onto the floor. Red Beard removed my gag.

"Welcome aboard the *Sinjoor*. You may shout all ye want, but no one'll hear ye!"

"I thought large ships couldn't reach Amsterdam because of the sandbars?" I asked.

"Aye, the large galleons can't. This ship has a shallow draught, and Capt'n knows the waters as well as his own knob."

The men left and shut the door. I heard the latch slide into place.

I sat in the darkness quietly. There was no point in yelling. No one would hear me. I thought of Nicolas and of La Rochelle. I thought of the day we'd seen the Musketeers arriving. How magnificent they looked in their finery. They were so strong, so sure of themselves. As the king's elite military unit, they were respected wherever they went … well, maybe not by the Huguenots …. But, I was sure that they were fearless and could do anything. I would never see Nicolas again. Then, I thought of Captain Carteret and the offer he had made. It was a chance for freedom and independence, not just an escape from becoming a stove-maker merchant. I'd a chance to explore the world and have adventures of my own but that had been taken from me too. I'd already learned a lot, but there was so much I still wanted to learn.

Then I thought of my père and *Maman* and Lidie and Mary. Papa refused to see what kind of a man Janssen was because of our great dependence upon him. *Maman* had known something was wrong. She'd just looked away. She said nothing! Just like she had always done. When Papa said we couldn't go and see Nicolas and his family any more, *Maman* had gone along with it. And when Louis had died, *Maman* had wanted to die with him. She couldn't even bring herself to care for Lidie or me. All she had to do was say something, and I wouldn't be here now!

I sat in the dark feeling abandoned and forgotten. Would they even miss me? Maybe I should have taken Captain Carteret up on his offer to make me his cabin boy. I thought of Captain Carteret. He had been nice to me, and patient.

The darkness and silence felt like a prison … no, a tomb. I was being buried alive, my dreams shattered. I sat in the darkness feeling the rocking of the ship and hearing the thudding of the seamen's footfalls as they readied the ship to sail. It all felt so pointless. Why would God make us leave La Rochelle, and everything I had ever known, for this?!

And then I thought of Job. God had blessed him with a wife, many children, servants, sheep, camels, oxen, and donkeys. Then on a whim, Satan asked to test Job's loyalty to God, claiming that he was only faithful because of all the blessings he'd received. So, God agreed, but said that Satan could not take Job's life. And so, Satan killed his servant, took his livestock, killed all of his children and then caused painful boils to cover his body. Job's friends told him that he must have done something wrong to be punished so, but Job said that no he did not do anything wrong. His wife told him to curse God and die, but he wouldn't do that either, though I couldn't understand why.

Why had God allowed such tragedy to befall Job when all Job had ever done was to worship Him? Why had God made us leave La Rochelle when Papa had always been faithful? Why did God allow me to be taken from my family and carried out to sea to work on a pirate ship when I had always done what my father had asked me to do? I had taken care of *Maman* and Lidie. I had gone to Protestant school, even when I didn't want to go. Yes, I had disobeyed and still gone to see Nicolas, even when I knew Papa didn't want me to, but he was still family ... and my best, my only, friend. He believed in God too, he just worshipped him differently. Louis ... was this my punishment for not watching Louis?

"I'm sorry! I didn't mean for him to die. I didn't want him to die. I was just so angry that I had to watch him again. I was angry that *Maman* was so weak. I'm sorry!"

I felt the tears stinging my eyes and tasted the salt on my tongue. I would give anything to bring him back.

As I sat in the dark weeping like a baby, I thought of something Captain Carteret had said.

> *"Etienne, you can't often control your circumstances, but you can control how you respond to them. Will you take control of the sails and determine your own course, or will you be carried away on the wind?"*

I decided then that I didn't want to be carried away on the wind. I would determine my own fate. I started struggling and working at the bindings on my hands. I scooted and wiggled until I was able to slip my hands around my bottom and slipped my feet through until my hands were in front of me. It was so much easier to do this time than when I had been trapped in that barrel! Thank you, François! Then, I used my teeth to work the knot. I could hear the sailors preparing the ship to take to sea. I worked faster. Finally, my hands were free. Then, I started working on freeing my feet. I could feel the ship rocking as the sailors loosened the moorings. I had to hurry! The ropes fell from my legs, and I leaped to my feet.

Now, to get out of this storeroom ... I felt my way to the door and rattled the handle. But it was as I feared — the latch was on the outside, and it was locked. I could see light filtering through the crack. If I could find something small, I just might be able to lift the latch, but with what? I searched the small room on my hands and knees for something ... anything, I could slip between the door and the jam. It was so dark ... I felt the ship bob and sway as it came free of the mooring. I didn't have much time left!

I felt boxes of apples and barrels of what I thought to be mead. There were bags of grain and large rounds of rye bread. I found salted meat and barrels of salted fish. There had to be something! Just when I was ready to despair, the floorboard creaked and moved. I felt along it and found a nail protruding from one end of the plank. I worked at it with my fingers until it started to move. Hurry. Hurry! It was already nearly too late. I ignored the pain in my fingers and willed strength into them.

I looked up and said, "If you give me the strength to pull out this nail and the ability to escape this prison, I will stop fighting your will and go where the tide takes me."

The nail came free. I moved cautiously to the door and listened. I couldn't hear anyone on the other side. I slid the nail into the crack between the door and the jam and lifted the latch. The latch rose, and, then, slipped off of the nail and back into place. I tried again, and, again, it slipped back into place. My heart was pounding in my ears. A memory of Captain Carteret trying to teach me Pythagoras's Theorem flashed before me.

Etienne, you must learn to calm yourself. Try it again.

I closed my eyes and took a deep breath, held it, and then released it slowly, like Captain Carteret had shown me, willing the tension to leave my shoulders. I opened my eyes and slid the nail into the crack again. This time the latch came free and flipped around. The door swung open.

I cautiously scanned the room. No one was there, I slipped out of the storeroom and quietly latched it behind me. I crept across the floor and up the steps to the deck. The sailors looked busy with the rigging. Perhaps they wouldn't notice me if I slipped out and dropped over the railing. The ship had left the dock, but it was still within easy swimming distance. There was still time. But just then the great white mainsail came down with a loud snap, and the ship began to move.

It had to be now! I bolted toward the deck rail, but as I did a burly sailor stepped in front of me grabbing at me. I darted to the right nearly running into another sailor who came up on that side. Sailors were appearing from all directions. I ran in the only direction I could — straight for the main mast. Without thinking I grabbed the rope ladder and began to climb. I climbed right up to the yardarm. I paused to look around. The ship was picking up speed, and the dock was slipping further and further away. It might already be too late. I looked down. Two sailors were starting up the ladder after me. I inched out onto the yardarm and carefully moved out along it. The men were gaining on me. I dropped down onto my hands and knees and continued to edge out along the beam. One sailor had reached the beam and was walking along it to me. I looked toward the dock. It was now a tiny spot on the horizon. I looked down to the dark water. How could anyone make that jump?

"Hold still boy. I'll get ye down." The sailor was nearly within arm's reach.

I remembered a story Maistre Quintal had told us from Acts 27, about when the Apostle Paul was taken to Rome as a prisoner and, when the ship got into trouble, the sailors wanted to kill Paul and the other prisoners.

"But the centurion wanted to spare Paul's life, and kept them from carrying out their plan. He ordered those who could swim to jump overboard first and get to land."

The sailor reached out for me. I knew what I had to do. It would have to be now or never. I took a deep breath, closed my eyes, and jumped!

Chapter 23

Baptism

It was a long way down. My stomach rose into my throat along with the panic. Then I hit the water feet first. The shock of it rippled from my ankles up to my knees and lower spine. Hundreds of icy pins pierced my body, and my muscles contracted with the cold. Then I heard a voice say, *"Breathe!"* I forced my lungs to expand just before I plunged beneath the water.

It was so cold and so dark. I plunged down, and down, and down. I felt like I was being buried alive. But I wanted to live. I started kicking and clawing my way up toward the light. My lungs burned. I kicked harder and struggled for the surface. I wasn't going to make it. But I had to! I thought of Magdalena and of Lidie.

I fought harder. The need to breathe was overwhelming! The water lightened. I was getting closer. Finally, when I thought I couldn't bear it any longer, my head broke the surface, and I sucked in a deep breath.

I looked around. The ship had taken the wind and was sailing away. In the opposite direction, the dock appeared as a dark streak way off in the distance. The water was so cold, so much colder than the water in La Rochelle. My body was already shaking.

The dock was too far away, and the ship was farther still, even if I resigned myself to return to it. I started swimming towards the docks: one stroke, two, three, four. I lifted my head to take a breath. Another stroke, two, three. The dock seemed no closer than when I started. I felt my legs going numb. I was going to die here in this place. I was angry; angry that we were forced to leave La Rochelle, angry that I would never see Nicolas again, angry with *Maman* and angry with my father. Why had I jumped off the ship to freeze and finally drown here? Where was God? Papa said that God would provide; but what had he provided? I had lost everything! I knew I would die there, alone.

I resigned myself to drown, and took one more look at the land, a parting memory. But the dock seemed closer now, so I kept swimming. Maybe I wouldn't die after all! Time seemed to stand still. I had to keep swimming. I was so tired. I could no longer feel my arms and legs. I looked up to see the dock. It was so close! Just a few more strokes …

I wasn't going to make it. I was barely moving now. So tired. I closed my eyes and felt the waves splashing into my face. It would be so easy to simply slip into the black and disappear. My head struck something hard. I forced myself to look up. The dock was looming overhead.

I'd made it! Somehow, I had made it. My arms shook as I pulled myself up. I rolled onto the deck and lay there trembling.

I felt hands shaking me. I opened my eyes and stared into Po's chocolate face. He looked scared and was breathing hard. Chloe was there too staring out at the ship I'd just left as it slipped further into the distance. Worry lines had drawn her brows together. She helped me up and wrapped a blanket around my shoulders. Slowly, she and Po helped me to walk.

"What are you doing here?" I asked.

"I saw them take ye." Po said in Dutch. "I told Ma and we came to find ye."

"Thank you!" I said and hugged him.

It was a long walk back to the doublewide townhouse where Lena was probably sewing in the sitting room; *Maman* was probably preparing food for supper; and where Lidie was playing with Mary. And my father? Would he be home by now? What would I do when I got there? Would Jacob Janssen van den Bergh be there? What would he do when he saw me?

As we approached the house, Chloe took me into the carriage house and Po helped me up the ladder on one end of the building into the loft where he and his mother lived. We came up onto a landing where a small door led into their living space. It was cozy and warm. There were two beds with straw mattresses, a small table with two stools, and two chairs set by the hearth.

Chloe gave me dry clothes to wear. Then she told Po to hide me there, and she would bring me something to eat. Po led me back out onto the landing. This time I saw that there was a narrow bridge leading across the open space in the center of the building to a railed loft on the other end of the building. This loft was filled with hay and straw.

Po led me across the bridge and secured me in a small open space behind the hay bales.

Po handed me a bladder of Meade. "Stay here. My ma or I'll come back when we can."

I waited through the remainder of the day. Chloe brought me a bowl of fish stew when her duties in the kitchen were finished. I lay in the hay through the night unable to sleep. I wondered if my parents knew what had happened to me. What had Janssen told them?

The next morning Po brought me rye bread and butter milk.

"Tell me," I asked in Dutch, "what do my parents know about me?"

"*Meester* said ye were sent to Texel. Ye'd return soon."

"So, they are not worried about me?"

Po shook his head. "'m sorry."

"Maybe I should go tell them I'm safe."

"No, that'd be bad. *Meester's* a'ways here. Him can't know you're here. He's dangerous. Please, stay quiet. He'll be leavin' in three days. Ye can come out then."

I spent the morning running scenarios. How could I get word to my family about what had happened without endangering them? Every time I thought I had found a solution, I then thought of something I had overlooked.

The afternoon wore on, and I began to imagine what it would be like to sail to distant lands with Captain Carteret. I knew that he had a home in New Netherlands, a Dutch colony in North America. I wondered what it was like. Did they have dark people like Chloe and Po living there too? Where else had he been? Then I remembered my bargain. I'd promised to go along with the tide. Did that mean that I would have to work with Papa as he wanted me to? I sighed.

I was restless and ventured out from behind the hay bales to peek out of the small window overlooking the garden. I saw *Maman* and Chloe outside the kitchen door scraping potatoes, presumably to add to the evening stew. Po was just outside the carriage house brushing the horses. I watched *Maman* take the potatoes into the house as Chloe took the scrapings to dump into the canal. As Chloe returned, Janssen came outside and said something to Chloe. Then as he approached Po, he looked up at the barn. I ducked down quickly and scrambled back to my hiding place in behind the hay. Had he seen me? I waited. All was quiet.

The light was softening, and I knew that evening was approaching. Po brought the horses into the carriage house, making soothing noises to them. He hitched them to the wagon, and I heard him talking to the horses a bit louder than necessary.

"Come beauties, time to get *Meneer* Gayneau, and bring him home." I heard him open the double doors that faced the street and canal that ran along the back of the property and lead the horses outside. Then the doors closed behind them.

The silence was unnerving; I hadn't realized how comforting it had been hearing the munching and neighing of the horses below. I was tired of hiding in the dark. I had to do something. I decided that it was safe to explore a bit and was starting to stand up when I heard an unfamiliar noise. Someone had entered the carriage house using the small door facing the house. It wasn't Chloe; her footfalls were light, barely making a sound, but these were heavy, as if made with boots. I heard them walk across the floor from the door to the garden. Then they paused and scraped the floor, as if their owner was looking around the room. Then they started up the ladder to the loft.

Who was this person? Why was he here? At least, I assumed it was a man. I risked a peak over the hay bales. It was Janssen, and he had nearly reached the top of the ladder! His back was to me as he climbed up the ladder on the far side.

I ducked back down behind the bales and tried to slow my breathing. Did he know I was here? I didn't think Red Beard could be back yet, so he shouldn't yet know I was missing, but then he might have seen me in the window. Why was he here? What would he do when he found me?

I heard him enter the room where Chloe and Po lived. Their space was small. It wouldn't take him long to search it, then he would come over here. Should I try to escape now? Would there be time to reach the ladder and get down before he came back out? No. He should be done searching their room any minute now.

I listened. It was so quiet. What was he doing? Why was he taking so long? Maybe I could say that Red Beard had thrown me overboard, hoping I'd drown? But why would he believe me? Why would Red Beard disobey orders like that? What was taking him so long?

Then I heard the garden door open again. Someone else entered the carriage house and closed the door gently. The foot falls were soft, almost silent. Chloe. I should warn her. But how? Any minute Janssen would come out and see me.

I heard her cross the floor and start to climb up the ladder. What would he do to her if she caught him in the act of searching for me? I readied myself. I would have to warn her. But then, this was her living space. She had a right to be here. How would he know she was helping me? I sat back down and tried to stay calm.

Chloe reached the top of the ladder and entered her room. I strained to listen. How would Janssen explain his presence in her room? But I heard nothing. There was some movement. I heard the boots crossing the wood floor. Then there were rustling sounds. I could hear voices, but they were so low I couldn't make out what they were saying. More rustling. Then silence.

They were in there a long time. I was starting to doze off, when I heard boots crossing the floor. The door opened, then closed, and he started down the ladder. I listened in surprise. I had expected him to come searching for me. I listened to him crossing the floor below then leaving through the garden door.

He must not know I was missing yet. But in that case, why had he come here?

Then I heard soft foot falls coming over the bridge. Chloe looked over the hay bales at me.

"How are ye doing?"

"I'm well. But why did Janssen come to see you?"

"Don't ye be worr'in 'bout that now. I don't think he knows that ye've gone missing yet. Ye'll need to stay put a couple more days."

I sighed. "Okay."

"Don't be tellin' Po of *Meester's* visit. I don't want him to concern 'imself."

I nodded.

"Be patient, lad, this'll all be over soon."

But it didn't seem like it to me.

The sun had set, and darkness spread through the carriage house. Po returned with Papa. I wanted to call out to him, to tell him I was here. How would he respond? He didn't know who Janssen was, or he didn't want to. He'd just let Janssen's men take me. Would he believe me, or would he be embarrassed and tell Janssen where I was? I stayed still.

A few moments later, Po came up the ladder and found me.

"Come, Etienne." Po led me across the bridge to the room where he and him mother lived and pushed open the door. "It's okay. No one is looking for you," he said.

Chloe arrived with two wooded bowls full of fish and potato stew. She set them on the table, while Po pulled one of the chairs by the hearth over to the table. He motioned for me to sit. Chloe went to an open wooden shelf by the hearth and pulled a small bowl down from it. She brought this to the table and spooned some of the stew from each full bowl into the empty one. The she offered me one. We all sat down to eat. I'd had the soup before, but this soup was excellent, better than I could remember it being before. Chloe offered me a piece of hard bread to sop up the remaining liquid in the bottom of the bowl. After supper, Chloe offered Po and me a cup of warm milk from a pot she'd hung over the fire.

"Ye will sleep with me tonight," Po said, pointing to his small bed. His smile glowed white in the dimness of the room.

I smiled back and nodded. It would be nice to sleep in a bed, rough as it was, instead of shivering in the hay bale alone.

"But in morning, ye must hide again," Chloe said, watching me, until I nodded my assent.

That night I dreamed of Louis.

It was my birthday and Louis was a baby. Papa gave me a satchel with nine bowling pins and the small leather ball. He'd whittled the pins out of hard wood, sanded and oiled them. I think he'd bought the ball from a street vendor I'd seen often near the plaza. Maman had sewn the satchel. I took each one out and ran my hands over the smooth surface. They were 9 inches tall, slender at the top and slightly bowed out at the bottom. They were beautiful! The ball was oiled leather and fitted nicely into the palm of my hand. I tossed it up gently, catching it again. It had a nice heft to it. I smiled.

"Thank you!" I hugged Papa and then Maman.

I showed the ball to Louis. He took the ball and tried to shove it into his mouth. Drool ran down his face. The ball dropped from his hand and landed on the floor with a thud. Louis giggled and reached out his hands to me. I picked up the ball, scrunching my face as I felt the slimy drool on it, and handed it back to him. He giggled again and took it eagerly. I was happy ...

I awoke and remembered where I was. Po was asleep beside me. I put my arm protectively around his shoulders and fell back to sleep.

The next day passed much like the first. I spent the day hiding among the hay in the loft daydreaming and listening to the noises around me. Po brought a light lunch around noon, and shared it with me, before returning to his duties. I'd gotten used to working, and the boredom made me restless and irritable.

Sometime in the late afternoon, I heard men talking in the yard and crept out from behind the hay bales. I moved to the loft window and peaked out.

Janssen was talking to Red Beard in the garden. He looked angry. He must now know of my escape. Maybe he would think I had died. I watched as Red Beard nodded and left. Janssen turned and walked back toward the house.

I waited until he had entered the main house. Then, I climbed down from the loft, crept to the door of the carriage house, and peered out.

I jumped as someone grabbed my arm. I spun around. Po.

"No go. No safe. Wait."

I shook my head. "I can't. Don't worry."

Po continued to hang onto my arm, trying to pull me away from the door.

"Please, stay!" He said. I could see the worry in his eyes.

"I'll be careful," I said, trying to be reassuring.

I opened the door a little wider and stuck my head out, looking both ways. I didn't see anyone, so I started walking towards the house, keeping to the perimeter of the garden. As I passed the elm tree, I heard the garden gate open, and dropped down on my belly behind a low hedge. I peered through the branches, trying to see who it was. I saw one black boot and a wooden peg leg. Red Beard! He started down the path and headed towards me. I lay as flat as I could and forced myself beneath the shrubbery. Branches tore at my clothes and poked painfully into my side and back.

I heard his uneven steps coming closer. They stopped on the other side of the hedge. I willed myself to be small, quiet, and unseen. I could hear him shifting his weight slightly as he waited, listening. I was acutely aware of a particularly sharp branch japing painfully into my side. I longed to move, or to grab it and break it off. But if I did either, Red Beard was sure to hear me. I willed myself to remain still. I tried to keep my breathing shallow and quiet. The wait was interminable.

"Are you needing something, Sir?" A soft voice said in Dutch. It was Po. He had come to my rescue again.

Red Beard grunted. "No. I'll be on my way." I heard him walk away.

I was just about to move, when Po's chocolate face leaned into mine. "Safe now."

I exhaled with relief and rolled out from under the bush. I stood brushing leaves off of my clothing. I smiled at Po and hurried to the back door of the house. I crept into the kitchen and peered around the door into the sitting room. *Maman* was sitting by the large hearth darning socks. Papa had gone off to work.

I watched Janssen as he read to Magdalena. He looked like any other loving father. And, yet, I now knew his darker side. I tried to think of what to do. I supposed I could keep hiding in the carriage house. Janssen would leave eventually for his next voyage. How much longer would that be? Chloe had said three days. It'd been two. One more day wasn't much, if she was right. If not … I couldn't hide forever. I knew Chloe and Po would help me; still, it was unlikely I would get away with it for much longer.

Chloe walked into the kitchen. She saw me and brought her hands to her mouth. I saw panic in her eyes. She moved towards me quickly and tried to pull me away, just as the back door banged open.

"Ah ha! Caught ye, ye slippery seal," he called.

Chloe's arms wrapped around me protectively, as Red Beard lunged for me. Janssen came into the kitchen, followed by *Maman* and Magdalena.

Red Beard had a firm grip on my arm and Janssen's eyes threw daggers at me.

"Oh!" Lena cried, seeing me and ran towards me.

"Get back child," Chloe told her gently. "Po take Lena into the other room."

I hadn't even seen Po, who slipped out from behind Red Beard and went to take Lena's hand to lead her away. Lena refused to move and looked from Red Beard to her father.

"What is wrong, Papa?"

I could see Janssen opening his mouth to respond, but then he closed it again with a sigh. *Maman* moved over to join Chloe by my side, keeping her eyes on Red Beard.

A banging on the front door broke the tension.

"Chloe, please answer the door," Janssen said.

Chloe hesitated and looked at *Maman*, who nodded almost imperceptibly, and went into the living room. Janssen gave a signal to Red Beard to keep us quiet and left to meet the visitors. Through the cracked door I could see two official-looking men pushed their way into the house.

"Jacob Janssen van den Bergh, we are arresting you on the charge of piracy."

At the sound of this announcement, Red Beard bolted for the back door and Lena ran into the living room. *Maman* pulled me into a tight embrace.

"You are accused of selling slaves in the Dutch colony of Berbice, in northern Brazil, without a license from the West India Company."

"*Niet mijn vader.*" Lena said, running over toward her father.

"Leentje …" Janssen tried to reach for his daughter, but the men held him back.

"*Maman*, I'm fine. Let go," I said as gently as I could, yet I heard the urgency in my voice.

I saw Chloe take hold of Lena, as the officials bound Janssen's hands and drag him outside. I freed myself and hurried into the living room just in time to see the officers loading Janssen into a waiting jailor's wagon. They locked him inside and drove away.

"This is your fault!" Lena yelled at me, bursting into tears, and running from the room.

Chapter 24

Goodbyes

Following the arrest, I'd felt an uneasiness and uncertainty, despite the fact that no one had seen Red Beard again. Everyone seemed somber and withdrawn. Lena would not talk to me or even look at me. Papa went to work as usual, but he did not ask me to go with him. *Maman*, Chloe, and Po went about their chores quietly. I had been left alone to do as I pleased. I'd reviewed everything I'd learned in my notebook several times by now.

On Sunday, two days after the authorities took Janssen away another man came to the door. We had just finished eating and had all settled down in the sitting room, when we heard the knock at the door.

"Uncle!" Lena said, laying down her stitching as Chloe let the man into the room. She ran into his arms. "Papa has been arrested. Chloe took me to see him, but they wouldn't let us in."

"*Ja,* they refused me also. He is to be tried within the week."

"What will happen to him then?" Lena asked, weakly.

Her uncle looked grim and shook his head slowly in answer. He put his arm around her. "I have come to take you home with me."

"Why?"

"You must be looked after in the event that … you cannot stay here alone."

"But I am not alone. The Gayneau family is here, and Chloe and Po … please, let me stay here."

"It is not possible. If things go badly, your father's property will be confiscated, and you cannot be here when they come. Chloe and Po will come with us." Then he turned to my father and said, "I strongly advise you to find other accommodations. I cannot guarantee what the outcome will be. There are rumors that the VOC is rounding up anyone they suspect of aiding my brother. If you stay here, you will be in danger of arrest."

"Thank you for the warning," Father said.

The man nodded and turned to Chloe, "Go and pack whatever things you have into the wagon. We'll meet you out back when we're ready to go."

She nodded and left the room.

Then turning to Magdalena, he said, "Come, we must pack your things."

Lidie burst into tears and ran out of the room. I went after her and found her in our little room behind the kitchen. She was in our bed sobbing into her doll. I sat down beside her and put my arm around her. She turned and flung her arms around my neck, sobbing into my shoulder.

"Why do they have to go?" she said between sobs.

"Janssen has gotten himself into trouble, and his brother has come to take care of Lena until he can get out of it."

"Why can't we go too?"

"We aren't her family."

"Chloe and Po aren't her family either," she said, stubbornly.

"They are the Janssen's servants. They are bound to them."

"Aren't we their servants too?"

"It's different with us. We voluntarily came to work for Janssen and have been paid for our work. Our term of service is over. Chloe and Po do not have a choice. They have been purchased for much longer terms."

Lidie sat up, and I wiped her face with her apron.

"I'll miss them."

"I will too," I said. Then, I noticed the satchel lying on the floor near our trunks. One of the nine pins was poking out of the top. I looked at Lidie. She sniffed and clutched her doll to her chest. "Go see if *Maman* needs help with Mary. I have something I need to do."

She nodded and slid off the bed. I followed her, grabbing the satchel as I did so. As Lidie went into the front sitting room, I went out into the back garden to look for Po. He wasn't there, so I headed to the carriage house. The horses whinnied as I entered. I went over to stroke their noses. Po was readying their harnesses. I watched as he led one horse over to the wagon and hooked him up. Then he came to get the one I was stroking, the one with the star on her nose. She nuzzled my hand, looking for a treat. Po held out a carrot, and she took it eagerly.

I looked at Po. His eyes were watery. I held up the satchel and handed it to him.

"For you."

Po took it tentatively and looked down at it. Then he burst into tears. He wrapped his arms around my waist, and I held him, gently patting his back. I looked up to see Chloe watching us. I expected her to yell at Po, but she didn't. She just stood there grim-faced.

Finally, she spoke, softly. I heard Po's name, but couldn't understand anything else.

Po pushed away and looked up at me. "Thank you," he said, holding the satchel tightly. "Sorry, must go."

I watched him lead the horse away and hitch it beside the other one. As I returned to the main house, I thought of Louis. Only this time, I didn't push the thought away.

Louis was laughing. It was the first time he had knocked the pins down by himself. How happy he'd been. He'd taken my hand and pulled me over to see what he had done. I'd smiled at him and reset the pins. Again, he'd thrown the ball and laughed as the pins skittered across the stone tiles.

I nodded to myself. Yes, it was the right thing to do. I know Louis would want Po to have them, someone who would enjoy them as much as he had. I wiped away a stray tear and entered the house.

Lena and her uncle were coming down the stairs. Her uncle carried a large trunk and Lena was dressed in the fine gown her father had given her. Her eyes were red, as if she had been crying. I followed them into the front sitting room.

"Good-bye, Lidie. I will miss you." Lena said, giving my sister a tight squeeze. Then she hugged *Maman* and kissed Mary's forehead. She curtsied to my father. Her eyes found me and then looked away. She darted out of the room.

"Magdalena, where are you going? We have much to do."

She returned quickly, carrying the potted tulip I'd given her.

Lena moved as if to pass me, but then gave me a quick hug and a kiss on the cheek.

I felt her slip something into my hand as she hurriedly followed her uncle out the door. Then, she was gone, and I hadn't even told her good-bye. I just stood there like a fool, while she disappeared into the carriage, and I didn't know if I would ever see her again. I opened my hand and saw the pink hair ribbon folded there. Why was this happening again?

I followed my parents in silence as we walked back to the church for the evening service. I sat through its entirety hearing nothing but the pounding of my heart. Then it was over, and we stood to leave. As we made our way to the back of the church, father stopped to speak with a group of several men. I recognized two of them from La Rochelle, the fathers of Paul Philippe and Jean, and there was a Dutch-looking man that I did not know.

"Is there still room for us?" Father asked as he approached them.

"There is, but we need to know your intentions now. There are two ships harbored in Texel. We must be ready to board tomorrow or Tuesday latest."

"We will be ready, but I don't yet have enough to cover the fare."

"That is no problem, friend," said the Dutch-looking man. "There are several passengers from Beest, who have asked the company to cover their fares until after we arrive in New Amsterdam. They will work off the debt once there. I am certain the captain will agree to extend you the same terms."

Papa sighed and nodded. "Very well then. We will join you in Texel on the morrow."

"Look for the ships the *St. Jan Baptiste* and *De Vergulde Bever* (*The Gilded Beaver*)."

My father nodded, and we walked home to prepare for yet another voyage. We were leaving Europe, and I knew, then, I would never see Lena, or Po, or Nicolas again.

Amanda M. Cetas

Part 3, The Voyage

May 9, 1661

Sailing the Atlantic from Amsterdam to New Netherland

Have I not commanded thee? Be strong and of a good courage; be not afraid, neither be thou dismayed: for the LORD thy God is with thee whithersoever thou goest. — Joshua 1:9

De Vergulde Bever (The Gilded Beaver) (1660), by Hendrick Cornelisz Vroom, Rijksmuseum, Amsterdam

Chapter 25

The Gilded Beaver

The harbor at Texel was bustling with activity. Slowly, we made our way through the crowds looking for some sign of the ships we were to take to North America: The *St. Jan Baptiste* and *De Vergulde Bever*. I was fascinated by the sight of four sailors carrying a large barrel, which was slung from ropes and held up by boards on each side between the men. I was amazed at how the men balanced the boards on their heads, rather than on their shoulders, as I had seen done in La Rochelle. Suddenly, my father stopped, and I nearly walked into him.

"Greetings, Brother Gayneau."

I looked up to see François and his father standing before us and sighed. I hoped they would be traveling on a different ship.

"Greetings, Brother Lefévre. It is good to see you. We are looking for *The Gilded Beaver*."

"You have found it, or at least the registry for it. We were told to sign the ledger and pay our fare, then they will load us onto row boats to ferry us out to the ship."

Papa nodded. "Is your good wife traveling with you?" he asked.

"Yes, she is resting with the younger children in the shade, just there," Brother Lefévre pointed to a shaded area near a building across the way. "Perhaps your wife would care to join her?"

"Oh yes, thank you. We have walked quite a long way," *Maman* said.

"Etienne, take the trunk over for your mother to sit upon."

"François, help him," Brother Lefévre said.

Before I could object, François took up one end of the trunk, and we followed *Maman* and Lidie across the crowded dock. Our mothers embraced each other, then *Maman* sighed deeply and relaxed onto the trunk. I was left to follow François back to our fathers.

"How did you like Amsterdam?" François asked.

I shrugged in response.

"Paul Philippe, Jean, and Jacques are here too, but I didn't see you at school."

"I was helping Papa with his work. He was injured, and, so, I needed to help."

"Ah yes, so you had said before. How could I have forgotten that you are only a *prolé*. Don't worry, we will have lots of building for you and your father to do in America. Perhaps, we will have you build our house for us."

Why couldn't I ever be rid of François and his friends? I slipped my hand into my pocket and closed my fingers around the little musketeer figurine. If I'd stayed with Nicolas, I might have been fencing now, instead of having to suffer François's taunting. Then I felt the silk ribbon tied around it and thought of Magdalena. How was she faring with her uncle? Another friend I would never see again.

We rejoined our fathers just as Brother Lefévre reached the small table. A ship's mate sat behind it supervising the signing of the ledger.

I watched as the men conversed and François's father counted out the required fare. The ship's mate made a note in the roster and waved him on. Then it was our turn.

"Name?" the ship's mate asked.

"Etienne Gaynaeu."

I watched as the man wrote "ESTIENE GENEJOY" in his large ledger.

"From where do you originate?"

"La Rochelle, in France."

The man wrote "from Rochelle" in the ledger.

"Who are you bringing with you?"

"My wife and three children," then he gave our ages.

The ship's mate wrote it all down in the ledger. "The fare is 108 florins."

"I have no money left after purchasing our supplies." Father spoke so softly I could hardly hear him, and I was standing next to him.

"No money?" The ship's mate asked, too loudly. My father visibly shrank and hung his head. "Then sign the ledger for credit. We will expect repayment in two years' time upon reaching New Amsterdam."

"Thank you," Father said. "You have my word on it."

We rejoined *Maman*, Lidie and François's family just in time to be escorted to the pier. There, we were lowered into a small boat and rowed out to the ship. As we approached one of the large, three-mast galleons moored in the deep waters, I could see the words painted on the back of the ship in gold lettering, *De Vergulde Bever*. We had reached the ship that would be our home for many weeks to come. I felt a growing sense of foreboding, as if this Gilded Beaver would swallow me whole, like the great fish that swallowed Jonah, only to be spit out on some distant, hostile land, from which I would never return.

After climbing on board, François and his family were shown to a cabin on the lower deck. Then we were led down to the cargo deck where screens of wood and canvas divided the space creating some limited privacy for the families residing here. The ship's mate showed us to one of these small spaces.

The ship stayed in port for two more days as it continued loading on people and supplies. Finally, on Thursday, the 12th of May, we set sail. Papa and *Maman* were anxious to get underway — the sooner to be done with the ship, I supposed. I would rather stay in Amsterdam. I thought of Magdalena again and touched the silk ribbon in my pocket as I watched the coast slip by and fade into the distance.

The next day, *Maistre* Evert Pietersen, a mousy-looking man, who held the position of Comforter of the Sick, Lay Reader, and School-master, called all of the youth to meet by the main mast for lessons. The morning was sunny, and it was hard to concentrate on the lessons. Instead, I watched the shipmates going about their business tending to the sails and tying off the ropes. I imagined myself commandeering one of the small boats and rowing back to port. I didn't know how I *would* find her, but I would find her.

"Etienne. … Etienne, that is your name is it not?"

I was jolted back to the present. I heard something hit the deck. I looked at Mr. Pietersen. "*Oui, Maitre.*"

"I do not know where you were just then, but I will expect your attention in future."

"I'm sorry, *Maitre.*"

Mr. Pietersen stared at me a long time, and I shifted my feet. What did he want from me? I wished we had never left La Rochelle.

"Go and join your friends. I expect I will not have any more trouble with you?"

"No, *Maitre.*" I turned to go and saw François holding something in his hand. He watched me and held it up to show me. I caught a glimpse of pink. I thrust my hand into my pocket. It was not there …

"It seems our *prolé* has a girlfriend." François taunted.

"Give it back!"

But François held it above my head jerking it away each time I reached for it. I suddenly felt possessed. I was hardly conscious of what I was doing. I watched myself punch François in the nose and felt the impact. The others joined in, but I had become a wild man. I had completely lost control. I saw glimpses of François, Jean and Jacques. I was aware that I was swinging both arms and was somehow fending off all three of them at once.

Then strong hands were pulling me off of François.

"Enough!"

The voice was commanding, and I dropped my arms. I looked up into the face of the stern ship's first mate.

"The four of you follow me."

In silence, I followed him with François and the others to the officer's quarters. When we got there the first mate commanded us to empty out pockets onto the table.

François launched into an explanation claiming that he had no idea why I would attack him and his friends. When he was finished the first mate turned to me.

"What have you to say for yourself?"

"I was trying to get my things back. François took my musketeer and ribbon and wouldn't return them."

The officer saw the figurine wrapped in pink lying on the table and picked it up. "Then this is yours?"

"Yes, Sir."

"We were just playing," François said. "We didn't mean any harm."

Then the officer saw my letters and picked them up. He unfolded the first one, and I watched him read. He looked me up and down. "All of you wait here," he said and left.

We stood in awkward silence. Finally, the officer returned with the ship's captain.

"This is Ship's Master Pieter Reyersz."

"It seems you boys were caught fighting on my ship. That is unacceptable. Which of you is Etienne Gayneau?"

"I am, Sir."

"According to this letter from Master Carteret, he has started training you as a cabin boy. He says that you showed an aptitude. But how am I to believe him after this incident? You have not made a good showing of yourself here."

"I'm sorry, Sir," I said, studying my worn shoes.

The master then turned to François. "You say that you were only playing, but it did not appear so to my first mate. And, so, to impress upon all of you the seriousness of your actions, you will report to the first mate at the main mast at dawn on Monday and work for him for a week. You will follow his orders or else you will be lashed."

"Yes, Sir," we all said, nearly in unison.

"You are all confined to your quarters until then."

As François passed me, he leaned in close and whispered in my ear, "Watch your back, *prolé*."

I took a deep breath to calm my nerves and started to follow the others out, but Master Reyersz stopped me.

"These are yours?" Master Reyersz held out my letters and the figurine, wrapped in the ribbon.

"Yes, Sir."

"When you are finished working for the first mate, you are to report to my quarters. Do you understand?"

"Yes, Sir." I sighed.

"You are dismissed."

Slowly, I walked back to our makeshift room. What was Papa going to say? He would not be happy. I wished I could melt away into the woodwork and disappear.

"Where have you been?" Papa asked without looking up from his reading, as I moved aside the curtain to enter our small quarters.

I looked down at my feet. How was I to begin? "I was held back to … I had to talk to … the captain."

"*Maistre* Pietersen told me you were fighting. What were you thinking? Don't you understand that we are here by the grace of the captain? We might just as easily be tossed off at the next port. Why would you endanger your family in this way?"

"I'm sorry, Papa."

The uncomfortable silence stretched between us, as I stood rooted to the floor fighting back tears. *Maman* stretched out her hand and softly laid it on Papa's arm. He met her eyes and sighed.

"Come and sit, *Garçon*. Tomorrow is a new day."

Chapter 26

Duties

François, Jean and Jacques were already clustered near the main mast when I arrived just after breaking my fast on Monday morning. I was happy to see the sky after two days of confinement. A fresh breeze filled the sails, and the sailors were hurrying about their business. It smelled like rain was coming. Finally, the first mate arrived scowling and looked us up and down.

"Four of ye, eh? Well this is your lucky day. You two," he said pointing to Jean and Jacques, "start aft. Pick up these brushes and buckets and wait for me at the back of the ship. Understand?"

They both nodded.

"Then off with ye. You two pick up these buckets and follow me." He turned on his heel and moved toward the bow of the ship.

Why did he have to pair me with François? Either Jean or Jacques would have been better. It was going to be a long week.

"You boys are in charge of keeping the *beakhead* and the chains clean. You will use these brushes to scrub the decks, the railings, the anchor chains and inside and around these holes. Use these ropes to tie yourselves to the *bowsprit* so you don't fall off."

"What is the beakhead?" François asked.

"It is this pointed area in the front of the ship. And the bowsprit is this horizontal mast that juts off the front of the ship and holds the foremost sail, known as the bowsprit yard."

"And what are these holes used for?" François said, pointing at the two square holes in the deck. There is one on either side of the bowsprit.

"Those are the latrines," the first mate answered, with a look of restrained humor "One for each of ye."

I examined the holes. A few dark lumps littered the deck around the openings and brown smears streaked the inside walls of the latrines.

"I am *not* cleaning that!" François said, crossing his arms over his chest.

The first mate just looked at him. "Ay, ye'll do it. And ye won't eat or sleep 'til it's done."

"You can't make me! My father won't let you."

The first mate just laughed and left us to our work. I wrapped the rope around my waist and used the bowline knot to secure myself to the bowsprit. It was the same knot I tried to teach Lidie back in Amsterdam. It was a stable knot and held fast when taunt, but when slack, it could easily be untied. I started scrubbing the deck. But François defiantly stood leaning against the rail with his arms crossed.

By midday, the first mate brought me salted pork, hard bread and mead. He brought nothing to François despite his complaints. Then the first mate inspected my work pointing out several places he wanted me to clean more thoroughly before he left to check on Jean and Jacques.

"Do my work for me, and we'll be even," François said.

"Even for what? What have I done to you?"

"You got me in trouble on the ship we took to Amsterdam."

"You did tie me up and put me in the barrel."

"It was just a game. I would have come back for you."

"But you didn't."

"You still gave me up to the Captain, and that is unforgiveable."

"Couldn't we just be friends, and forget all of the past slights?"

"No, we couldn't, *prolé.*"

I shrugged. "I don't have time to do both my work and yours."

"If you don't do my work, you'll be sorry. I will make you pay for it when you least expect it."

"Why do you hate me so much?"

"Why are you a *prolé?*"

"Do your own work," I said.

The sky was now overcast and ominous. Rain was coming. The latrine was the last thing I had to clean. All day sailors had come to use it, squatting over the hole to do their business. There were no privacy barriers and the sailors seemed to have no need for modesty. It was messy business, and now I must clean it up. The first mate returned, just as I was finishing up. But, the first mate made it clear that I was *not* done. He lowered me into the hole so that I could clean beneath the bow.

I could see the waves splashing up against the bow far below. It was a long way down. I hoped I had done an adequate job on the knot. I finished up and the first mate hauled me up, just as it started to rain.

My work was done, but François had not yet started his. The rain was coming down in earnest now.

"The work is not done. No one leaves until the work is done," the first mate said.

"But I have finished my half. François didn't do his work."

"No one leaves, and no one eats or sleeps."

It was not fair that I should have to do François's work too. But the alternative was stay in the rain and the cold all night. So, I grabbed the brush and started scrubbing the deck. François stood his ground. The first mate remained, with arms folded, leaning against the bowsprit.

I heard footfalls approaching and looked up to see Brother Lefévre.

"Why is my son still here? It is dark and wet; he will catch his death."

"No work, no food, and no sleep," the first mate replied.

"You cannot keep him here."

"*Ja, Meneer*, I can."

"I am a paying passenger … "

"With nowhere else to go. Whom will ye tell?"

"I will go to the captain."

"Then go."

Lefévre watched us for a moment and then stomped off, presumably to find the captain.

It made no sense to scrub the deck in the pouring rain, but I kept at it. I could feel eyes watching me. A few moments later Lefévre returned. I could hear François shift his feet. I looked up in time to see him flash a self-satisfied smile, but, before he could say anything, his father walked up to him and hit him across the face with a loud, wet smack.

"Get on your knees and help Etienne scrub the deck boy. Now!"

The extra work was worth the look of horror that crossed François's face. I quickly looked down at my work before he saw the satisfaction on my own face. François finally picked up his bucket and dropped to his knees.

My fingers were numb, and I was soaked to the skin and shivering, when we finally finished. My back and neck hurt, and my arms and legs were trembling uncontrollably. Lefévre grabbed François roughly by the arm and dragged him off. I collected both buckets, and the first mate showed me where to stow them.

The first mate squeezed my shoulder as I headed back to my

make-shift cabin. "Tomorrow, same time."

I nodded and stumbled down the stairs.

François was already on deck with his bucket and brush when I arrived the next morning. I noticed that he was moving stiffly, as if in pain, but at least he was ready to work. As I knelt down beside him, the ship slid up on the surf and I stumbled into François.

He winced. "Watch it, *prolé*!"

Again, I thought that it was a waste of time to clean the decks after last night's steady rain. They looked cleaner than I had seen them since boarding, but I dared not say so to the first mate. Today we were told to clean the main deck. It was a massive task that required several full days to complete. By evening, the fog, had rolled in, blanketing the deck, as François and I stowed our buckets and brushes away. The fog stayed through Wednesday morning too, making our work harder. I heard some of the sailors murmuring.

"Bad luck's coming," said one.

"Aye, better keep a close watch tonight," said another.

"What do they mean by that?" François asked.

"Just superstitions," I answered.

"Well, I don't like it either," François replied and continued scrubbing with added fervor.

On Thursday morning, I saw land to the west of us.

"What land is that?" I asked a young cabin boy who happened by us. He looked to be about my age, though he was shorter. He was fair, with long blond hair tied at the nape of his neck. He had an air of confidence and authority.

"That's Buchan Ness, it's just off the coast of the Orkney Islands. We have to sail north around them to get out into the Atlantic." He studied me. "Who are you? I haven't seen you at lessons."

"Etienne Gayneau. I'm a passenger."

"A passenger, eh? Wha'd'ye do to earn this detail, then?"

"Fighting."

The boy chuckled. "I'm Jan. Captain Pieter Reyersz is my uncle. My father is the captain of *De Vergulde Otter.*"

"Pleased to meet you."

Jan smiled. "See you around."

By afternoon, the wind was gaining strength. François and I were finishing the main deck when I heard the alert. The waves were growing in strength and size. I quickly secured a rope to my waist and threw another to François.

"Tie yourself in!"

But François was staring motionless toward the bow of the ship. I looked up and saw a large wave rising before us. It hit, sending water flooding across the deck. François lost his footing and slid across the deck, crashing into the main mast.

I ran to him and tried to grab the rope from him. He wouldn't let go.

"François let me help. Let go!"

A shadow fell across us. Another huge wave rose above the bow. I caught another rope, or what sailors called a *sheet*, hanging off the main mast and ran it around him. My hands fumbled with the knot. It suddenly got dark. I forced my hands to work the bowline on a bight … the fox comes out of the hole around the double trees, crosses under its trailing tail and out to its ending. The wave crashed onto the deck. François was ripped away from me. I struggled to hold my breath as the water tumbled me over and over. I crashed into wood. The railing … I reached out and slammed into it again. This time I hung on. I felt the urgency to breathe. Cold air hit my face, and I sucked in a breath, as another wave crashed onto the deck.

I thought of François. Did I tighten the knot enough? Was he okay? I couldn't see him. Water swirled over the deck. Men were yelling. I looked up to see men hanging from rope ladders trying to lower the *mersseijlen*, the top sails. Where was François? I looked around, squinting into the mist. Something moved by the main mast. It was François. The sheet, from the lowered sail, or *yard*, was flapping in the wind not far from me. I used it to pull myself over to the dark lump by the mast. Another wave crashed onto the deck. Again, I was pulled away.

The ship was rocking violently from side to side as the helmsman tried to keep the bow pointed into the waves. Finally, the last of the yards were lowered, and the rocking was somewhat less violent. I crawled over to François. His mouth was gaping like a fish just pulled from the water. He wasn't breathing. I hit him on the back — hard. He leaned over and retched onto the deck. I touched his shoulder, but he jerked away and retched some more.

"Leave me ... alone ... *prolé* ..."

He could be a little bit grateful, I thought. Maybe I should have left him to ... but a pang of guilt filled me. Well, he could clean up his own vomit.

Another shadow fell over us. I looked up to see a sailor climbing down the rope ladder above us.

"What are ye still doing here?" he bellowed, trying to be heard above the howling wind. "Get below decks!"

I untied myself and tried to help François. His eyes just stared, unfocused at his feet. I gave up and started toward the stairs. But the sailor called me back. He deftly released François from the yard and pulled him to his feet.

"Help him to his quarters," he said, draping François's arm over my shoulder. I staggered a step to regain my balance. The bow started to pitch upward again, and we hurried below decks before another wave could wash us off the deck.

"There you are! Tell me a story." Lidie jumped up on the bed and wrapped her arms around my neck.

"Etienne, where have you been? I've been so worried. What's happening?"

"It's just a storm. Don't worry, *Maman*. The sailors know what they're doing."

"I just wish this infernal rocking would stop!"

Papa was lying in his bunk next to *Maman*. He appeared to be sleeping. His skin was pale and had a greenish caste to it.

Lidie stroked my hair and stared into my eyes.

"Was it scary? We heard a crash and water started seeping between ceiling boards. The water's cold."

"It was a little scary, but I was tied to a rope so I wouldn't go overboard."

"Like Jonah?"

"Jonah was thrown overboard; it was deliberate."

"Why? Why did the sailors throw him overboard?"

"Jonah told them to. He knew the storm was his fault, because he disobeyed God. God told him to preach to the people in Nineveh and tell them to repent. But he didn't want to and ran in the opposite direction. So, God punished him by sending the storm."

"Is that what God is doing now? Were we supposed to stay in La Rochelle or Amsterdam?"

"No, Lidie. I don't think we're being punished. It's just a storm. Go to sleep. It will be better in the morning."

The words rang in my ears. They were the same words, the same sentiments, Papa used with me. First, when we fled La Rochelle, then in Amsterdam and again, after my fight. But was it better? I thought of Nicolas and Magdalena.

I rubbed the silk ribbon between my fingers and felt the solidness of the wooden musketeer. Once again, we were headed out into the unknown. What would we find in America? What kind of people lived there?

Chapter 27

A Birthday Surprise

Today was Friday, May 20th, my tenth birthday. The storm had continued through the night. By dawn, the stench of sick was overpowering. *Maman* was already up, doing what she could for Papa, who was sicker than she was. Water still leaked through the cracks in the boards above us. It must still be raining. It was unlikely the first mate would need me today, but one never knew and, anyway, I had to get out of this confinement.

I started up the stairs to the deck, careful to keep a hold of the railing. As I emerged onto the deck, I saw the waves breaking against cliffs off the port side. They looked dangerously close.

"What are you doing above deck?" Jan asked, grabbing me by the arm.

"What's going on? Aren't we getting too close to the breakers?"

"Aye. The wind is blowing from the NNE and is pushing us in. Every time we try to push around the Orkneys the winds push us back into the Moray Firth. So now we're just trying to stay off the rocks. Pray the wind changes soon.

"What are the Orkneys?" I asked, my eyes fixed on the waves breaking against the rocks.

"They are a group of islands, located off the northern tip of Scotland. And the Moray Firth is the large bay off the northeast corner of Scotland. We could try to sail between the Orkneys and Scotland, but it is too dangerous. There are too many rocks under water for a ship of this size. It's best to go around them. But with these winds … it'll be safer if you stay below deck until the weather calms."

"I came up to get a bucket of water."

"Hurry then."

I found a bucket and brush and held it out as a wave crashed onto the deck. It was filled in short order and I returned below deck.

Maman was wiping Papa's face when I entered our makeshift quarters. Without a word, I started cleaning up the mess. *Maman* sent Lidie for Mr. Evert Pietersen. Papa didn't look at all well. I took the soiled bucket up to the deck and dumped it over the side, rinsed it, and refilled it. The ship had made no progress. All the sailors' efforts were in trying to keep the winds from pushing us closer to the shore. I returned below.

Mary was squalling in her basinet. I went over and picked her up. "Shush now little one. It'll be alright."

Mary stuffed her fist into her mouth and whimpered softly. Lidie returned then with *Maistre* Pietersen. He looked harried and tired. He felt Papa's head and the back of his neck.

"Has he eaten anything?"

"Not since the storm began."

"Any drink?"

"We tried to give him mead, but it all came back up," *Maman* said.

"He seems to be severely seasick. He does not have a fever. Many others are suffering likewise."

Then *Maistre* Pietersen bent down, pulled a ceramic jar out of his bag and opened it. He took out, what appeared to be, a bit of reddish-brown clay and smeared it under Papa's nose.

"The best remedy I have is to keep a piece of Earth under the nose. I will return later, when it dries out, to replace it."

Maman sat next to Papa stroking his head. Lidie took Mary from me and sat on the floor to play with her. No one seemed to notice me. So, I decided to go in search of Jan.

The rain had stopped. I heard the bell ring ... one ... two ... and headed in that direction toward the upper deck ... five ... six ... Jan was holding the half hourglass in one hand and ringing the bell with the other ... eight. Eight rings, one for each half hour of the watch. It was time for the changing of the crew.

"Still overcast. Can't measure the latitude again today," Jan said, as I approached. "But they'll still take the speed. Do you want to help with it?"

"*Oui ... ja,*" I replied.

I followed him to the officers' quarters where he traded the half hourglass for the half-minute glass.

"Take this and follow me."

We marched to the back of the ship timing our footfalls to the lurching of the ship. A couple of sailors were preparing to cast the log line off the back of the ship into the water. One sailor held the reel, and the other prepared the log. The log was a weighted piece of flat board on which was tied a rope. Knots had been tied along the length of the rope line.

"When you hear the splash, turn the glass over. When the last grain runs out, call stop." Jan instructed.

The sailor counted out the knots as they ran through his fingers.

"Stop!"

"Eight!" the sailor replied.

"We are making top speed," Jan said. "Average speed is between 4 and 5 knots. We'd best go tell the captain. He'll be pleased to hear we are making up for lost time."

Jan knocked at the door and then entered without waiting for a response. Captain Pieter Reyersz looked up from his desk as we entered.

"Eight knots, but still no latitude," Jan reported.

The captain nodded. "Etienne Gayneau, our first mate tells me that you worked hard and were proficient in your duties. That's good to hear. I will honor Master Carteret's request to continue your training on this ship, should you wish."

"Yes, Sir. Thank you, Sir."

"You will work with Jan. He will teach you to use the instruments and take the readings. You will also shadow him when he has the watch. *Begrijp je dat?*"

"Yes, Sir, I understand. Thank you, Sir."

"Do you have a compass rose?"

"No, Sir."

"Here, take this one. It is yours to keep."

The captain handed me a small wooden box. I lifted the lid and stared at the compass. The brass casing was polished to a bright shine. The red and black triangles, which radiated out from a center rose in the eight primary directions, were easy to read behind the glass face. I watched the needle spin until it settled in one direction. I remembered that Captain Carteret told me the arrow always pointed north, so I rotated the compass until the arrow fell on the boldly printed *Noorden*. The compass was so beautiful! I couldn't believe Captain Reyersz just *gave* it to me. I swallowed and remembered my manners.

"Thank you again, Sir!" I said, mortified to hear my voice crack.

The captain smiled. "I have many others. Your first job is to learn the 32-points on the compass."

"Come on. I'll help you," Jan said, leading me over to his bunk in the officer's quarters. We worked diligently until evening.

Night fell, the wind picked up again. As I left Jan to return to my quarters, I saw sailors scrambling to take in the sails.

"See those sails, they are the *schooverseijl* and *fock*. The *schooverseijl* is the main course sail; it is the lowest sail on the main mast. The *fock* is the foresail; the sail at the front of the ship. You'll have to learn all the names of the sails too."

I looked around. There had to be nearly a dozen sails.

"Don't worry, I'll help you with it later," Jan said and laughed.

I recited the directions as I walked. The eight main points were easy: *north, northeast, east, southeast, south, southwest,* and *west.* I learned those under Captain Carteret. It was the directions in between that were difficult: *north by east, north northeast, north east by north* and so on. Why does *north by east* come before *north northeast*?

Maman had some rye bread, salami and cheese for me when I arrived.

"How were you all today?" I asked.

"Mary crawled," Lidie said, sitting beside me on the bunk.

"We'll have to watch her closer from now on," I said.

Lidie just sat there, watching me.

"How's Papa?"

"Sleepy. *Maman* kept putting the Earth under his nose."

"He is still not eating, but we got him to drink a little diluted mead. And it stayed down," *Maman* said. "Perhaps the bit of Earth is helping. Mary is finally asleep. You should go to sleep too, Lidie."

"*Oui, Maman.*"

Everyone had forgotten that it was my birthday. I held the wooden box carefully and traced its contours with my finger. I did get a birthday gift, though.

Chapter 28

The Watch

Jan and I were on watch Saturday morning. The wind and the waves were high.

"Etienne, look! See there is our companion ship the St. Jan Baptiste. It's being pushed into the bay."

I took the looking glass Jan handed me and peered into the lens. It was surprisingly difficult to locate the ship. I had to keep spotting it with my own eyes and then searching in that area with the spyglass. Finally, I saw it. The ship looked small buffeted against the waves. Suddenly, the foresail ripped off its sheet and flew out into the cliffs. The ship lurched and disappeared into the rising fog.

"What happened? Where did it go?" Jan took the spyglass from me and scanned the horizon.

"Their foresail blew off. It looks like they are getting pushed into the breakers."

"That'll be our fate soon enough, if we don't correct our course." Jan said, and hurried to the bell and began ringing it vigorously.

The captain and first mate came running. Jan explained what we had seen.

"Did you see the *St. Jan Baptiste* hit the rocks?" Captain Reyersz asked.

"No. I saw the foresail ripped away and the ship disappeared into the fog."

The captain instructed the first mate to have the crew fire the cannon.

One shot was fired with a loud boom. We waited ... no response. Another shot was ordered. Again, we waited and again there was no response from the St. Jan Baptiste.

The sea had become tumultuous. I thought of Papa and *Maman*, who was caring for him.

"Tie in! Tie in!"

Jan and I each grabbed the closest ropes as an ominous shadow crossed the deck. I looked ahead to see a wave rising up to touch the heavens and worked to secure myself to the sheet. Jan was already yelling orders to the other sailors, having tied his knot in half the time it took me. I pulled the rope as the wave crashed onto the deck.

My feet were swept out from under me, and I slid across the deck until the rope stopped my progress. Air. I breathed. Dark shapes loomed to port side. We were nearing the cliffs. Men scrambled up the ropes to lower and secure the sails. Another wave rose up before us.

I thought of Jonah. How did he have the courage to tell the sailors to throw him into the sea? I hadn't prayed in a long time. I prayed now. *Please God, don't let us end up on those rocks. Protect this ship and everyone on it.*

By the next morning, the sea had calmed. I was again on watch with Jan. There was still no word from the St. Jan Baptiste.

"Look over there," I said pointing. "I thought I saw something."

Jan looked through the spyglass. "Ships. Three of them."

"What kind of ships are they?" I asked.

"Don't know yet. Could be whalers … or pirates. They don't look like merchant galleons."

Pirates. I felt a shiver run down my back. I remembered the corsairs in La Rochelle. They were men to be feared. They frequented the taverns and drinking houses near the outer port, in the shadow of the lantern tower, where, ironically, many of them might later be imprisoned.

Throughout the watch, the ships approached slowly. What would happen if the pirates boarded us? Would they take us as hostages, or simply kill us? They would take our ship and valuables for sure. Should we fight? I thought of Nicolas and his fencing lessons. But I didn't have a sword. What good would I be in a fight? Would they spare my family if I volunteered to join them? It was a fearful thought. Was survival preferable? Or death?

One of the ships hailed us. The captain hailed them back and pre-pared to receive them.

"Why is the captain letting them board?" I asked Jan.

"Why not?"

"Shouldn't we fight? What of the women and children?"

Jan looked at me and started to laugh. "They aren't pirates. They're *seesekruisers*, warships hired by the VOC, the East India Company, to protect their merchant ships."

I felt the heat rising in my face.

"Come, Etienne," Jan slapped me on the back. "Let's go meet them."

Captain Reyersz greeted the officers as they came aboard. "Have you come across any other ships in the area?"

"No. You're the first."

"We've lost sight of our companion ship in the storm and fear she may have been drawn onto the rocks."

"We've not seen her, but we'll keep an eye out. Where are you bound?"

"New Netherlands. And you?"

"We're waiting for our ships returning from the East Indies. We'd expected them by now, but with the storm … they're likely detained."

"Aye. We've lost three days already trying to round the Orkneys. Each time we get close the storm comes up and pushes us back to the Moray Firth."

"I wish you fair weather, then. We'll keep an eye out for your companions. Good luck to you. And keep an eye out for pirates. They're thick in these waters."

Pirates …

The bells announced that it was noon and time for the changing of the watch.

"Sun's out. Come on, I'll show you how to find the latitude," Jan said, heading to the officer's quarters. "Have you ever used a back-staff?"

"No. Captain Carteret used an astrolabe. I never did understand how it worked."

"They're much more complicated," Jan said. "The English developed the back-staff, but we call it the English Quadrant. It's much easier to use. You don't have to look at the sun with this like you do with the astrolabe or the croft's staff."

The back-staff consisted of a long-graduated staff, a shadow arc on one end of the staff with a larger sight arc on the other end. A brass horizon vane was at the far-end of the staff and a slit for the sight vane at the fore-end of the staff.

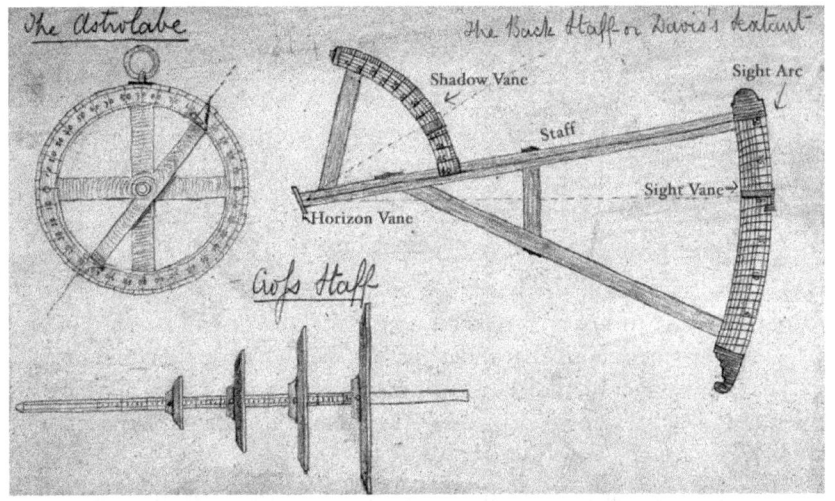

Navigation: An Astrolabe, a Cross-staff, and a Back-staff or Davis's Sextant.
Drawing after Edmund Gunter, 1624.
Black & white and labeled. Welcome Collection
Creative Commons Attribution only license CC BY 4.0
http://creativecommons.org/licenses/by/4.0/

I watched Jan hold the staff by the sight vane with his back to the sun. He held it up so that the sun cast a shadow on the shadow arc, while he looked through the sight vane keeping it level with the horizon. He made some adjustments and made a note in the logbook.

"Now you try."

I turned my back to the sun and held up the staff, as Jan had done.

"Now, line up the horizon vane with the horizon and slide the half-staff back and forth until the shadow of its vane falls across the slit in the bottom. Make sure the horizon is still visible through the slit."

We determined the latitude to be 58°59'. Wind was from the west northwest. Captain Reyersz set our heading for north by west.

Papa was sitting up in bed when I returned for supper. He even managed to eat some bread.

"*Garçon*, how are your studies going?"

"I've learned all the headings on the compass, and, today, Jan taught me how to use an English quadrant to determine latitude. We also saw three warships this morning too, but we've lost sight of the St. Jan Baptist. We're afraid it might have gotten caught on the rocks, but we don't know for sure. Captain Reyersz said we'll look for it for a few more days."

Papa's face turned serious. "Then we must pray for the ship and all of those on board."

Papa took *Maman*'s hand, and she took mine. I grabbed Lidie's hand, and she completed the circle with Papa. We bowed our heads while Papa prayed.

Afterwards, Papa said, "I am sorry that we missed your birthday, *Garçon*."

"It's okay."

"I have something for you." Papa reached into the large trunk and pulled out a small package wrapped in butcher paper and handed it to me.

I felt through the wrapping and made out a handle. It could be a blade, but it was too small to be a sword. I opened it cautiously. It was a hunting knife with a smoothly polished wooden handle. Images of reindeer, moose and a bear were burned into the leather sheath. There was a loop to fix it to my belt. I pulled the knife loose and felt the blade. Sharp!

"Thank you, Papa!" I laid the knife down and put my arms around Papa. "I love it!"

"I thought you could use it where we are going."

What will this new world be like? As I lay in the dark waiting for sleep, I thought about what it would be like in this new place. I imagined myself walking along a beach with wild grasses swaying in the breeze. I could smell the salt in the air. No one else was in sight. Suddenly, a bear stood up on his hind legs in front of me. He was so tall he blocked out the sun. He growled, and I grabbed my knife circling it cautiously. It dropped to four paws and followed me. I was wary, studying his movements. I stared at the bear, refusing to back away. I slowly crouched down, and sprang at the bear ...

Captain Reyersz spent six more days looking for the St. Jan Baptiste, without success. On the 28th of May, he finally gave the order to continue the journey and sail on around the Orkney Islands. Then, yesterday, Tuesday, the 7th of June, the weather was clear enough for Jan and me to take the reading for latitude. Jan recorded in the ledger, 48°17' and 12 knots for speed. Then together we recorded our bearing on the map. I had noticed then that within one day we would reach latitude 46°10', nearly back to La Rochelle, where my adventures had begun.

Today, I was standing on the upper deck on the port side staring off into the distance. All I could see was water, but I kept hoping to spot land. It was too cloudy to determine the latitude, but from Jan's and my estimates, the ship should be just about parallel to La Rochelle, La Ville Blanche. I squinted into the distance trying to see the limestone façades glowing in the bright coastal sunlight. But of course, we were hundreds of miles out to sea. ... What was Nicolas doing now? Did he ever find out what happened to us? If I wrote him a letter, how would he receive it?

"You might be able to see it if you climbed up to the crow's nest." Jan said as he leaned on the railing beside me.

"See what?"

"Don't be coy with me, Etienne. I know you miss your home. I still miss mine ... sometimes. Especially, my mother. I'll see her when we get back, but I still miss her."

"At least you will see her again. I don't know if I'll ever see my cousin, again."

"Write him a letter. When I get back to Amsterdam, I'll find a ship going to La Rochelle and have them deliver it to him."

"Really, you would do that?"

"Of course."

"Maybe you could deliver one more letter, to my friend in Amsterdam?"

Jan gives me a strange smile. "Sure, I'll find her for you."

"I didn't say it was a girl."

"You didn't have to. I've seen you playing with that pink ribbon when you thought I wasn't watching." Then he slapped me on the shoulder. "Your secret's safe with me."

Then I remembered Jacob Janssen's story about the baptisms.

"Are we likely to get near the coast of Portugal?"

"Why do you ask?" Jan said, watching me curiously.

"I heard a story about the Dutch seaman's baptisms off the Berlingues and was wondering if we would be passing them."

Jan grinned. "The slavers' ships sailing to Africa or other ships sailing into the Mediterranean Sea pass by that way. We will be well out into the Atlantic when we reach that latitude. There is no need to practice your diving on this voyage."

I sighed, relieved.

Jan laughed and slapped me on the back. "Come on, it's time to ring the bell for the changing of the watch. You can do it this time."

Just then I saw a flash of light in the distance. I grabbed the spyglass and scanned the horizon. There it was again. I thought I saw sails. The specter danced just out of view. I called for Jan.

"What did you see?"

"I thought I saw a ship over there," I pointed. "Just on the horizon."

Jan took the spyglass and scanned the horizon.

"Are you sure?"

"Yes. I mean, I thought I saw something."

"Keep looking and let me know if you see it again."

The skipper approached and handed me a small bundle.

"What's this?"

"Stores are getting low. That's your food ration for today. Keep your eyes sharp. You see any fish give a holler. It'd be nice to do a bit of fishing right about now."

I opened my bundle to see a 3½-piece ration of bread and cheese to last all day. No salami or dried beef. No salted pork. I sighed and broke off a piece of cheese and a bit of hard bread. I could really use some soup or stew to soften it in. I saved half of my portion, tucking it into my jacket pocket.

Fish *would* be good right about now. I strained my eyes to watch for movement in the sea. The undulations of the waves played tricks on me. I would think I saw a fish jumping out of the water, only to realize it was just a wave. Then I saw the glint again.

"Jan, look over there," I said, handing the spyglass to him. It was a ship, much closer this time. There was no question.

"What flag are they flying?"

"I don't see a flag of nationality, just a plain black one."

"Go and ring the bell," he said calmly, but I could see the concern on his face.

Captain Reyersz hurried over. "What did you see, Jan?"

"Ship at two o'clock. Etienne spotted it. Looks like a 10-gun Brigantine."

The captain took the spyglass and scanned for the ship.

A Brigantine was a two-mast ship rigged with square sails on the foremast and gaff sails on the main mast. They were smaller than warships and galleons, but they were very fast and maneuverable. There was only one real purpose I could think of for a ship like that ...

Chapter 29

Trouble at Sea

The black ship was approaching swiftly to starboard, or the right side of the ship. I could see that the gun ports were open along the side of the ship. And, through the spyglass, I could see what looked like small cannons fixed to the ship railings. One of them fired a warning shot.

"Beat to quarters," Captain Reyersz commanded. "Hard to port! We're running."

Jan began ringing the bell vigorously, and the first mate started giving orders to the seamen. I watched the men scramble up the ropes to raise the topsails. The starboard side of the deck reared up as the great ship turned away from the approaching vessel.

The dark ship chased us all afternoon, creeping ever closer. As darkness fell, the captain called all the officers to his quarters.

"We need to lose the pirate ship by morning, or risk being boarded," Captain Reyersz said. "I'm ordering black out conditions on board. Cover all the windows and allow only minimal lanterns below decks. Make sure no light leaks through. No smoking on deck and no lights."

"But, Captain, it's a new moon. How'll we see to work?" asked the first mate.

"You'll have to make do. I don't want any spark to give away our position. Then, I want a change of course. I want a hard turn to starboard and a heading south southwest. We'll try to double back on our pursuers and slip by their spotters."

"We're approaching the Azores. Won't we be in danger of running into them?" Jan asked.

"If the readings are true, we should just manage to miss them. It's a risk, but we have to chance it," the captain paused and gave a half smile. "We'll see how accurate your calculations are, Jan."

Jan grimaced and shot me a nervous glance. I smiled encouragingly back.

"Oh, and one more thing. I don't want to hear any talking or sing-ing on deck and only whispers below deck. Spread the word. Nothing must give us away. This plan cannot fail."

We all nodded. The first mate left to inform the rest of the crew and passengers.

"Jan and Etienne," the captain said, taking us aside. "I need you both stationed at the furthest point on the beakhead to watch for breakers. They will indicate the presence of land," he added for my benefit. "If you see them, one of you is to run and tell rudder man. And be sure to note their position."

"How will we see them in the dark?" I asked.

"Even with the stars alone, there should be enough light to reflect off the white caps."

The meeting was adjourned, and everyone hurried about their business. Jan and I took up our positions at the beakhead.

A cold wind hit my face and found its way through my clothing, sending a shiver down my spine, though the temperature was still quite mild. The stars were bright in the cloudless sky, shedding a surprising amount of light. I wondered if the pirate ship would still be able to see us, despite blocking out the cabin lights.

What would happen if the pirates caught up to us? What if we ran aground at the Azores? Or even worse, we ran right into the pirate ship? I scanned the dark water for any sign of white caps, but there was nothing. The night stretched on and on. It was eerie. The creaking of the masts seemed extraordinarily loud. It felt like I was guarding a ghost ship. What would we find in the morning?

In the second hour of the watch I saw them, white caps breaking on unseen rocks. I called to Jan.

"Do you see the white caps off the port side?"

"Ja! Run and tell the rudder man."

I slid down the banister and ran across the deck. I reached the back of the ship and took the steps two at a time to reach the quarter deck.

"Breakers to port, maybe two, three yards out," I said, panting.

The rudder man nodded and turned the great wheel adjusting our path to starboard. I looked out behind us. There was no sign of the pirate ship. I rejoined Jan.

We watched the breakers slip past. After a while Jan spotted breakers to starboard. They were now on both sides of the ship. We must be sailing between islands. This time Jan ran to make the report. I watched as the ship slid through the inky water. If we moved too far to port or starboard, we would likely end up on the rocks.

We passed several tense hours straining our eyes to spot any impending danger.

As the dawn broke, the first mate approached us. "There's been no sign of the pirate ship," he reported. "Looks like we made it. We still need to keep an eye out but looks like the captain's plan worked. Go get some sleep. Someone will wake you in a few hours."

The feeling of relief was palpable on the deck. Men smoked and clapped each other on their backs. There was still a state of alert though, should the pirates reappear.

We passed the Azores on the 12th of June, but despite our best efforts there were no sightings of fish. Sixteen more days passed without success; it had been twenty since I strained to see La Rochelle on the horizon. Our food was nearly gone and drinking water was running low. The skipper was rationing each of us to one *flapkan*, or tankard, a day (about 2 pints or 1.5 liters). Yesterday, I spotted two *plysterten*. They were a type of sea bird notable for their long arrow-like tails. Jan said that this was good sign, as birds tend to follow schools of fish. It also meant that land must be nearby. So, today, Jan and I were doubling our efforts on lookout.

"Look who it is standing up there all high and mighty?"

Since serving my time with the first mate, I had done my best to avoid François, and, now, here he was looking up at me from the main deck flanked by his posse: Paul Philippe, Jean, Jacques and, his little brother, Tomas.

"I don't have time to spar with you today, François."

"No, you have to *earn* your passage, *prolé*. Come on boys, let's leave him to his duties."

Suddenly, a flying fish leapt out of the water, followed by a whole school of them. I ran to ring the bell. Sailors appeared from all sides to cast fishing lines and nets over the side of the ship. As I watched, a commotion erupted on the starboard side. Men were yelling and flocking together. I leaned over the top deck rail for a better look. A cry went out, and I saw a huge fish with a long-pointed nose, like a sword, flop onto the deck.

"Look, Etienne they caught a *Dratus*!" Jan said, coming up beside me.

But almost before the words left his mouth, there was a cry from the port side and a shark hit the deck with a thud. The shark was small, compared to the large man-eaters we often saw circling the ship in calm weather, though it was still larger than I was. A crowd grew around the shark as it thrashed its tail and snapped its jaws. Several men were attempting to club it on the head.

I glanced to starboard and saw Tomas approaching the *dratus*. The sailors had abandoned it to help with the shark. It lay motionless on the deck. I saw its tail twitch, just as Tomas reached out to touch it …

"No, Tomas!"

I was running. I slid down the stair railing and landed hard on the main deck, but I was too late! Tomas was screaming. The *dratus* had speared his hand with the point of its nose. I pulled my knife and drove it through the fish's head. It lay still.

"Hold still, Tomas!"

The boy was still wailing and holding the wrist of his skewered hand. I grabbed the wrist of his injured hand to hold it still. Then, I put my foot on the head of the fish and cut off its nose. Others had come running. A circle of sailors surrounded us.

"Tomas!" François pushed his way through the crowd. "What have you done to him?"

Tomas was sobbing.

François started to pull the sword-nose out of his brother's hand.

"Don't pull it out here, boy," a sailor said. "He'll bleed too much. It needs to be cauterized. We need to start a fire!"

Several sailors led François and Tomas off, leaving me standing by the dead *dratus*, alone.

Then a strong hand grabbed my shoulder. Captain Reyersz was standing beside me. "That was quick thinking, Etienne. You might well have saved that boy's life. You'll make a good officer someday. There's a place for you here, if you want it. Jan is quite fond of you."

Chapter 30

Scurvy

A few days later, Tomas approached me shyly.

"I want to thank you." Tomas held up his bandaged hand. "Mr. Pietersen said it would heal up nicely. If you hadn't had been there …"

"Tomas! What are you doing?" François grabbed his brother's good hand and pulled him away. "Why are you talking to this … *prolé* after what he did to you?"

Tomas looked back over his shoulder as his brother led him away. I smiled at him and nodded my acceptance of his thanks.

Over the next three weeks, I frequently caught Tomas watching me when I had my turn on the watch. One evening during the first watch, as the darkness settled in, Tomas approached me.

"You shouldn't be seen with me. What will your brother say?"

"François is sick in bed. He is weak, and he has red blotches all over his body."

"Sounds like scurvy," Jan said, coming up behind us "The voyage is taking its toll on the passengers. Many have started coming down sick. The fresh produce ran out weeks ago. With a bit of luck, they can all hold out another week or two until we reach New Amsterdam."

"Which way is the land?" Tomas asked.

"Look up at the stars," I said pointing to Polaris. "See that bright star? That's the North Star."

"I don't see it. Which one?"

"Do you see those bright stars that form a rectangle? Off the right end are three more stars that look like a handle."

"I see it. It looks like a big ladle."

"That's right. That's the constellation Cassiopeia, the big bear."

"Why is it a bear?"

"The handle of the ladle forms the tail. The rectangle forms the body. Then connect a few more stars and it is an upside-down bear."

"Oh."

"But that doesn't matter. Look at the bright star on the ladle rim opposite from the handle. Then follow that down to the next bright star. See it?"

"Yes."

"That star is called, Polaris. It's the North Star. So that way is north. That's the way we have to go now."

"How much longer before we find the land?"

"I don't know exactly, but we still have a long way to go."

"What will happen to François if we don't get fresh fruit soon?"

"He'll continue to get weaker and, eventually, he will die," Jan said, looking grim. "I've seen it happen more than I would like. We would've reached America by now, if we hadn't spent so long looking for the St. Jan Baptiste."

The three of us stood staring into the horizon as the silence stretched on.

"Don't be mad at François, Etienne. I know he can be mean, but he doesn't understand. He's jealous of you."

"Why would he be jealous of me?"

"You have a *père* that loves you and is proud of you. Our papa is so hard on François. He can never be good enough for Papa."

I thought back to the stoves I had to build in Amsterdam. I could still hear Papa's chiding to move the bricks just so. I was sorry that François's father was hard on him, but mine was hard on me too, and it didn't excuse his bullying.

I felt Tomas watching me, but I refused to look at him. He touched my arm lightly, but I just clenched my teeth and stared resolutely into the distance. There was nothing more to say. Tomas walked away.

When I arrived back at my cabin, *Maman* pulled me aside.

"I am worried about your sister, Lidie. She has been tired and dizzy all day. She won't eat. She says her teeth hurt, and I saw blood in her mouth."

I tried not to show concern on my face. "I'm sure she will feel better in a day or two, *Maman*. What do we have for her to eat?"

"Just salted fish and a bit of mead. The bread ran out yesterday."

"No fruit or vegetables?"

"No. They've been gone for weeks."

"I'll try to find something else tomorrow. How's Papa?"

"Weak. He is eating a little, but he's lost a lot of weight."

"Don't worry, *Maman*. It'll be alright." I stepped into *Maman*'s embrace and let her cry into my shoulder.

As much as I tried to reassure her, I knew that Lidie most likely had scurvy too, and we were nowhere near land. I thought of Louis. He had been my responsibility, and I had failed to keep him safe. I now felt responsible for my entire family. I mustn't fail again.

The next day, I searched every corner and crevice on the ship looking for anything to give Lidie, but there was nothing. The wind had died down, slowing our progress. Three more weeks passed before there were any signs of land in the distance. Lidie was weaker. She could no longer get out of bed. And deep red spots had appeared all over her body. Mr. Pietersen agreed that she had scurvy, and that she needed fresh fruit, and soon.

On Thursday, July 21, I saw a large sea bird. Jan called it a Jan van Gent (a Northern Gannet). There was still no sign of land, but Jan said they could forage up to a hundred and fifty miles from shore. Then, on Friday, the water changed, and I saw bits of vegetation floating near the surface. In one place, the water was as green as grass. Land must be close now. I prayed that Lidie could hold out a bit longer.

Finally, I saw land on the morning of Wednesday, July 27. I ran to tell *Maman*. Papa looked better, as if he could sense that the land was close. But, Lidie looked so frail. She couldn't die now, not when we were so close. I lay next to her and took her hand.

"We're almost to shore," I whispered.

"I'm so tired."

"I know, but you've got to fight a little bit longer."

"That's what Louis said."

"What?"

"Louis told me I had to live a bit longer. That land was close now, and that you would save me."

"Louis was here? When? How could that be?"

"You'll have to ask him." Lidie sighed and closed her eyes.

"But he's ... how do you know him? You were just a baby ..."

"I don't know, but it was Louis."

I wanted to ask her more, but she was asleep. It was some time longer before I too could sleep.

I awoke to a jolt that knocked me out of bed. I landed hard on the floor, as the ship listed to port. I dressed quickly and went in search of Jan.

Part 4, A New World

29 July 1661

Arrival at Manhattan Island, New Amsterdam in North America

Shew thy marvellous lovingkindness, o thou that saves by thy right hand them which put their trust [in thee] from those that rise up [against them]. — Psalm 17:7

A view of New Amsterdam from Governor's Island
Manhattan 1660, by Len Tantillo

Amanda M. Cetas

Chapter 31

Land

"We've run aground!" Jan said, as I approached.

"What does that mean for us? Are we stuck here? How far away is New Amsterdam? And how are we going to get there?"

"See that sandy peninsula that looks like a hook just off the port side?"

I looked to my left and nodded.

"That's Sandy Hook. It marks the entrance to the lower bay. We still have to sail through that opening straight ahead into the upper bay. It's still nearly 20 nautical miles from here."

I took the spyglass and looked off the bow of the ship. There, in the distance, I thought I saw buildings beyond the upper bay, but it might just have been my eyes playing tricks on me. I sighed. It would take a long time to row that distance. Suddenly, there was an ear-splitting boom, as the ship's cannon was fired.

"The captain is notifying the port that we need help," Jan said. "We have to lighten the ship, so we can refloat it. If we stay here too long, the waves will break us apart."

"Are they taking off the passengers?"

"More likely, they will unload the cargo."

A second volley from the cannon, rocked the ship. I had to find Captain Reyersz. I hurried below deck.

"Where are you going?" Jan yelled after me, but another boom of the cannon saved me the explanation.

I found the captain, just as the cannon was fired for the fourth time. The force of it nearly knocked me off my feet.

"Captain, may I have permission to disembark when the ships get here?"

"We will only be removing cargo. The passengers will remain on board. But once the weight is lightened, we will be able to continue on to Manhattan."

"But my sister has scurvy. I need to get to shore quickly to find fresh fruit for her."

"There are many with scurvy. We will be in port soon enough. There is nothing to be gained."

"But, Sir …"

"Enough! It wouldn't do to lose you in the last two days of our journey. What would your parents say?"

I returned to my quarters. Lidie wasn't moving. She was feverish, and I couldn't wake her.

"What's happened, Etienne?"

Maman was watching me intently. I told her of the beaching and the plan to unload the cargo first.

"I asked the captain to let me go with the yachts when they get here, so I can find some fruit and bring it back, but he won't allow it."

"Then we are nearly there?"

"Yes, *Maman*. But it could be a few days yet before we are able to disembark."

"Well, that is something."

"But Lidie's getting worse. We need to do something now!"

Papa sat up in his bed and looked at me. "*Garçon*, God has provided for us thus far. He will continue to provide for us."

"Maybe if you spoke to the captain, Papa, he would let me go?"

"We will wait. You'll see, tomorrow will be better."

Why did he always say that? When had tomorrow ever been better? We have had to flee for our lives twice, only to lose everything we had, twice. And now, Lidie is dying within sight of land!

"*Maman*, you agree with me, don't you?"

"Your father is right. God will provide. You'll see."

I looked at Lidie. Her breathing was shallow and labored. Sweat beaded her forehead. I remembered Louis again. I saw him climb over the low fence. I heard him calling my name as he ran to catch up to me … No, not again.

I slid my knife sheath onto my belt, grabbed my satchel, and went in search of Jan. I found him on the deck peering through the spyglass off the bow.

"The colonists have sent the yachts. They should be here in two or three hours."

I looked where Jan was pointing and barely made out the small, single-sailed boats in the distance.

"Jan, I need your help. I need to get to shore. Lidie is sick with scurvy, and I don't think she has long left."

"Have you talked to Captain Reyersz?"

"Yes. He won't let me leave with the yachts."

"So, you want me to disobey his orders?"

"No. I just want you to look the other way, for a minute or two, while I find a way onto one of those yachts."

"There is no way you can get onto the boats without being seen." Jan looked thoughtful. "Not unless you can't be seen."

"What are you saying?"

"Come with me."

Jan led me below deck to the cargo hold. He found a barrel that had been emptied of its contents and moved it to where the other cargo containers sat.

"Are you sure you want to do this? You'll be cramped inside for hours, and, then, you'll have to figure out how to get out when you reach land."

"I know, but I must do it."

"Then, we'll have to make sure the top is on tight enough that it will stay on and appears unopened, but we'll need to remove enough nails, so that you'll be able to open it from inside. You'll also want to have a cork you can remove if it gets too stuffy or hard to breathe."

We rolled the barrel over to a secluded storeroom and got to work. Jan found a corkscrew that we fitted to a cork plug and we installed in on the inside so that I could remove it, as necessary.

Then we decided on three shortened nails. The top would look secure, but it would be easier for me to punch it out. We were ready. Jan went up the ladder to check on the progress of the yachts. A few minutes later, he returned.

"They're nearly here. We'd best get the barrel in place and seal you in before the sailors come down to retrieve them."

We made sure to place the barrel at the front of the first load to go. I climbed in, and Jan nailed down the lid, then I waited.

The barrel had been used to store mead and still smelled of it. It felt like hours passed before I heard men talking. I felt the barrel being lifted and carried. Then, I was lowered and loaded into one of the waiting yachts. I could once again feel the rhythmic rocking of the tide and hear singing of the men as they worked. It seemed to take ages for the boat to be loaded. The wait was agonizing! Finally, we moved.

I tried to relax and hoped the tide was in our favor. What would this new place be like? It was owned by the Dutch, so I expected it to be more like Amsterdam. But New Amsterdam was located further south by latitude than La Rochelle, so the weather should be warmer.

The rhythmic rocking of the yacht was soothing, and I must have drifted off. I awoke to the sensation of being moved again. I didn't know how long I had been asleep. I was lifted off the boat and onto the dock. Then I was being rolled up a ramp. It was disorienting and made me dizzy.

Finally, the barrel was set on end with a thud. I found myself upside down on my head! The lid we'd so carefully rigged for easy removal was now firmly set against the ground. I felt bile rising in my throat and blood was thumping in my ears. How will I get out of here now?

I felt an urgency to get out the barrel. I'd have to try. Mustering as much force as I could, I kicked at the top of the barrel with both feet. It was solid. I kicked again, and again. It was hard to get much force, wedged into the barrel, as I was.

Please, God, help me!

I took as deep a breath as I could and kicked at the bottom of the barrel again, and then again. I felt it give a little bit. I kicked once more, and then again until I felt it give way. Then, I straightened my legs and pushed with my arms. The weight of the effort tipped over the barrel and I scooted out. As I stood up, several surprised men stared at me, but before anyone could stop me, I took off at a run toward the closely built rows of houses that lined the docks. The houses were made of yellow brick and had steeply peaked roofs. I cut down a wide lane and looked for a market or shopping district.

This town was far different than anything I'd ever seen. Where La Rochelle was so beautifully illuminated with its white limestone buildings, red tile roofs and archways lining the streets, this town's buildings were a riot of yellow colored brick and brightly painted wood. Where Amsterdam was well-laid out in orderly arcs of tree-lined canals and tidy homes, this place was a chaotic jumble of homes, taverns, brew-houses, shops and inns sporting signs with scantily-clad women, mugs brimming with ale, or beaver hides.

The people were different too. In La Rochelle, most everyone was French. The nobility was easily discernible in their grand finery from the merchant and working classes. In Amsterdam, the nobility dressed plainer, so that it was hard to tell one class from the others. Children there played games in the market squares, but there was a certain decorum in the adults. Here there seemed to be no social order or decorum at all. I saw men and women laughing together inappropriately in public view. I heard two other men yelling at each other, and there were all sorts of people here. Amsterdam drew people from all over Europe as well as ebony servants, like Chloe, but it was nothing like this place. There were Dutch and French and Swedes, judging from their tall stature and fair complexion. Two, I judged to be English and others German. There were also many with ebony skin and black-kinky hair. Magdalena told me they came from Africa. There were others with dark, reddish skin and long, dark-brown hair tied in braids or ponytails down their backs. They were strangely dressed too, wearing garments of soft leather tied with beaded belts. Their shoes were also soft leather. Were they the native people of this land?

I found a woman pushing a cart filled with cherries.

"May I have some cherries, please?" I asked in my best Dutch.

"Have you money?"

I shook my head.

"Come back when you do, and you may have some cherries."

I wandered the streets, but no one was willing to help me. Then, I remembered that Captain Carteret had told me that he grew cherries on his property in New Netherlands. But where was I going to find his house? I asked several people, but no one knew him. It must be late afternoon, judging from the sun's position. I started heading north out of town asking people about the captain as I went. A small man with spectacles and a large stack of ledgers was hurrying down the street toward me. He was muttering to himself, but I recognized the language. It was French.

"*Excusé moi.*"

The man looked up at me. "What do you want? I am in a hurry."

"Do you know a Captain Carteret?"

The man cocked his head and stared at me. "What do you want with him?"

I pulled his letter from my pocket and held it up to the man to read. "He brought my family from La Rochelle to Amsterdam and started training me to be a cabin boy."

"I know him. I am his bookkeeper."

"Do you know where I might find him?"

"You just missed him. He is likely well on his way back to France by now. Don't expect him back again until next year."

"Then do you know where I might find his house? He told me of his cherry trees. And my sister, well, she has scurvy. It doesn't look good. I need to bring her some cherries, but I have no money to buy any. I don't think Captain Carteret would mind if I picked just a few."

The man just started at me with furrowed brows. He looked at the letter again and then back at me. Finally, he seemed to come to a decision.

"His house is just over yonder. Follow the road to the top of the hill. It is the large, white-plastered house at the top overlooking the sea. You can't miss it. Cherry trees flank both sides of the house. A man named, William Palmer, is renting rooms in the place. Don't know if he'll be there, though. He's building a new ship down at the harbor."

I thanked him and started running up the road.

I found the house and knocked at the door. No one answered. I walked around to the first, large cherry tree closest to the house. It was loaded with fruit. I had to be careful to choose only the ripe, fully red cherries. I started picking the small fruit and dropping them into my satchel. I moved through the tree, climbing ever higher into the canopy, careful not to snap the thinner branches.

"What are you doing? Get down!"

Chapter 32

Cherries

I looked down to see a man dressed in an apron covered in saw-dust. He carried a carpenter's toolbox and stood staring up at me. I presumed that he was William Palmer, and started to greet him. But before I could explain myself, Palmer grabbed my foot and tried to pull me out of the tree. I hung on. When I refused to come down, he began to pick up oyster shells from a pile nearby and proceeded to throw them at me. I did my best to dodge the missiles without falling out of the tree. Finally, Mr. Palmer grabbed up a large measurement stick from his toolbox and began to wallop me. I dropped to the ground and took off at a run.

I heard footsteps crunching in the dirt road and looked up to see Mr. Palmer in pursuit. I ran back towards town.

"Thief! Thief!" Mr. Palmer was yelling as he followed me into town.

I tripped over a stone and felt Mr. Palmer's stick strike my side. I was breathing hard now, and I struggled to regain my balance.

Another crack of the stick, and I was driven to the ground. I struggled to stand, but Palmer grabbed me by the throat and tried to choke me. I twisted and brought my knee up hard. It connected, and Palmer groaned. I broke away and ran into a house, startling its occupants.

Mr. Palmer was up again and yelling. I saw Captain Carteret's bookkeeper running towards us, but Mr. Palmer rounded on the bookkeeper stick raised, yelling threats against me. I left the house to go to the bookkeeper, but Palmer prevented me. The bookkeeper quickly retreated.

Many people were now coming out of their houses to stare at Palmer, who kept screaming at me and beating me with his stick. No one, however, offered to help me. I cowered on the ground with my arms raised above me protectively. What would Nicolas have done? I thought of the Musketeer easily parrying my awkward attacks, but I didn't have a blade. Even a wooden practice sword would be useful to block the vicious strikes. All I had was my knife. I could maybe get in under his arm and stab it in his ribs … It was a sin to kill, but it would be in self-defense. I had just resolved to act when, the bookkeeper returned with the constable. The constable, with the help of several other men, grabbed Palmer's arms, restraining him.

"What is going on here?" the constable asked, looking from Palmer to me.

"This boy stole cherries from my tree."

"I just needed them to save my sister."

The constable looked to the bookkeeper who just shrugged.

"Hand over the cherries, boy."

"Please, can't I just keep them? My sister …"

"Don't make this worse for yourself. I should put you in the stockade."

Slowly, I handed over the satchel to the constable and stared at the ground.

To this Palmer responded, "Throw him in the stockade! There must be a penalty for stealing."

"No real harm's been done. Boy's learned his lesson."

"Is there no rule of law in this backwater outpost?"

"In point of fact, they are not even your cherries, but Captain Carteret's," the bookkeeper said.

"As his tenant, they are my cherries for the term of my lease!"

"That is an argument you both may bring before the Magistrate. For now, I am ordering you to go home and cool off, or else I will throw you in the stockades," the constable said. "You can appear before the magistrate in the morning to make your claim."

"Come with me, Boy. You will have to stay in the jailhouse tonight. Then the magistrate can hear your case tomorrow."

"No, I can't! My sister will die."

"Where is your sister?"

"She's on *De Vergulde Bever*."

"Is that the ship stuck on the sand bar?"

I nodded.

"There's nothing you can do for her tonight. This way."

The constable led me to a small jailhouse and locked me in one of the small cells. He gave me some water and a small loaf of hard bread. How could this situation get any worse? I remembered the last time I had been confined on Janssen's ship, and, then, I thought of Job again. Was I going to lose my sister now, just as Job lost his whole family? I wondered again, why God would allow innocent people to die?

It was stiflingly hot. I felt helpless as I sat down on the hard bench. It was going to be a long night. I tried to sleep, but I couldn't stop thinking about Job. No matter how bad it got, he never cursed God. Why not? His friends accused him, telling him that he was being punished for something he had done, but Job said he had done nothing wrong. Still he praised God even when he thought God had abandoned him. Why? He did question God. What had God answered?

I could almost see Maistre Quintal's animated oration, voice thundering, as he reached the climax of the story. God had listed out all of the great wonders of creation and asked Job if he knew how they were formed, how to control each element, how to feed each wild animal. Job did not know all the many things that God does.

I could see the stars through a small window high in the wall. I saw the stars forming the constellation of Orion. God had asked Job if he could loosen Orion's belt, and, of course, Job couldn't. God had reminded Job of how powerful he was with all of the things He could do, and how fearful He was. God had asked Job if he could instruct the Almighty God or correct Him. Job couldn't, but instead acknowledged that God can do anything and knows everything, and no one is wise enough to advise God.

A shudder ran through my body and I bowed my head, remembering God's assurances to Jeremiah to return Jerusalem to the Israelites after the Chaldeans had captured the city and exiled its people.

"Yes, I will rejoice over them to do them good, and I will assuredly plant them in this land, with all My heart and with all My soul." For thus says the Lord: "Just as I have brought all this great calamity on this people, so I will bring on them all the good that I have promised them."

The air had cooled some overnight, but it didn't help me to sleep any better. I'd eaten the bread as the sun had set, but that was hours ago. I had tried to sleep, but all I could think about was Lidie lying in her bed. I supposed Père and *Maman* were also wondering where I was.

As the sun rose, lighting my dark cell, I began to pace. It seemed hours before the constable finally came to escort me to the courthouse.

The magistrate was seated behind a tall podium raised up on a platform. He wore a black robe and a white-powdered wig. He banged his gavel as I was led into the court room.

"What are the charges?"

"This boy is accused of stealing cherries from Captain Carteret's estate yesterday evening," the constable said.

"What is the evidence?"

The constable approached the magistrate and laid my satchel with the cherries on his podium. The magistrate looked inside and frowned.

"Is Captain Carteret present?"

"No, Sir," the constable answered.

"Then, who brings the charges?"

"I do!" William Palmer said, standing up.

"And who are you?"

"William Palmer. I am renting rooms in Captain Carteret's house. I caught the boy in one of the cherry trees filling the satchel, then I chased him back into town."

"Where you very nearly beat him to death," the constable added.

The magistrate sighed and looked at me. "What do you have to say for yourself?"

"My sister has scurvy. She is near death. So, I smuggled myself off *De Vergulde Bever* with the cargo to find fresh fruit to take back to her, but I didn't have any money. I remembered that Captain Carteret had told me about his house here and his cherry trees. I didn't think he'd mind if I took some."

"Does Mr. Carteret captain the *Gilded Beaver*?"

"No, that is Captain Reyersz."

"Then, how do you know Captain Carteret?"

"I served as his cabin boy from La Rochelle to Texel. Here is the note he gave me." I offered the letter, and the constable took it to the magistrate.

The magistrate took the letter, opened it, and read it. "He speaks highly of you, Etienne Gayneau." He folded the note and handed it back to the constable. "But you still didn't get direct permission from Mr. Carteret or his tenant, William Palmer?"

"Captain Carteret told me about his home and his cherry trees. He said I should look him up, and that I would have permission to pick his cherries, should we ever come to New Netherlands," I answered.

"Do you have anything in writing?"

"No, Sir."

The magistrate looked from me to Mr. Palmer and back again. "I order you to return the cherries to Mr. Palmer, and, then, you are free to go your way." He brought the gavel down with a thump.

"I protest!" Mr. Palmer said, jumping to his feet. "He should be thrown into the stockades for thieving, and on a Sunday too! He is a *Papist!*"

The magistrate thumped his gavel several times. "My decision stands! Control yourself Mr. Palmer, or I will hold you in contempt."

The constable removed my shackles and handed me back my letter and satchel. I poured the cherries into the basket he held out for me. I watched as the constable handed the basket over to Mr. Palmer. I sighed and left the courthouse.

The morning bustle was in full swing in the market. I was tired and looked for a place to sit on the edge of the market where I could think what to do. A shadow crossed my face and I looked up to see the old woman watching me. It couldn't be … I blinked and looked again. It was the same old woman who had helped me in Amsterdam. She smiled and nodded to me. She turned and pointed to a slender, young native girl coming down the road with a bundle of furs on her back.

I stood up and walked towards her. She watched me approaching and sized me up and down.

"Are you lost?" she asked in Dutch.

"No, but I need help. I need cherries to give my sister. She's sick, but I have no money."

The girl studied me thoughtfully. "My name is Alsoomse. It means independent. My mother says it has always been so. Even as a child I would not listen to her." She laughed.

"My name is Etienne. I am named for my father and his father before him."

She smiled. "Give me your belt, Etienne."

"My belt? Why? It is not valuable."

But Alsoomse just waited. Finally, I took off my belt and handed it to her. Then she took off her belt. It was beautiful, made of shell beads. She handed it to me. I slipped it through the loop of my knife sheath and tied it on.

"Now we are allied," she said. "We are friends. Wait here."

I watched as Alsoomse took a small animal fur out of her pack and walked over to the woman with the cherries. Alsoomse returned with her deerskin skirt full of cherries. She filled my satchel.

"Thank you! But I have nothing to give you for them."

I was ashamed. What would my father say if he knew I had indebted us again? I stuffed my hands into my pockets, and my hand closed around the small musketeer wrapped in the ribbon – Magdalena's ribbon. It was all I had to remember her, but Lidie needed the cherries to live. I took a deep breath and pulled out the figurine. I unwrapped the pink ribbon and offered both items to Alsoomse.

I saw a smile form on Alsoomse's lips. She carefully took the ribbon and felt its silky texture. I watched her use it to tie back her hair. Then she took the figurine and turned it over in her hands.

"What is this?"

"It is a musketeer, a warrior, from my country. I had wanted to become a musketeer someday. But I will never be able to train for it now."

"We will see, Etienne. There are many kinds of warriors. Where is your sister?"

"She is on a large boat, stuck on a sand bar in the bay."

"Like that one?" Alsoomse said, pointing out to the water.

I looked up and saw our ship *De Vergulde Bever* anchored in the bay. "They made it in!"

"How did you get to shore, if not on your ship?"

I told her about being smuggled in the barrel.

She laughed. "That is why you smell like a sailor who has drunken too much firewater!"

I felt my face flush.

"Go take the cherries to your sister."

"But how will I find you again?"

"I will find you. I will return when I have more beaver skins to trade." She smiled. "We will see one another again."

I watched her disappear into the crowd.

Chapter 33

Forgiveness

I ran to the docks and found a boat just arriving. I waited as the sailors helped their passengers out of the boat. They lifted out their trunks and other personal belongings and prepared to return to the ship.

"Wait! Are you going to the *Beaver*?"

"Aye."

"Take me with you. I have family on board."

"Then why aren't you with them?"

"They're sick. I came to find fruit for them."

"Hurry then."

I jumped into the boat and took a seat in the middle, holding my satchel close. Now the trick was to get back on board without the captain seeing me. I was not sure what he would do if he knew I had so blatantly ignored his orders.

Jan was there to greet me on the deck.

"Hurry, the captain is preoccupied just now, but he could be back any minute."

I quickly climbed onto the deck. "Do you know if François and his family are still on board?"

"Aye, they are. The captain is only unloading the cargo and healthy passengers. The sick will be moved after the doctor has assessed their condition to ensure they do not have a contagious disease that requires they be quarantined."

I nodded and hurried to find François. I didn't know why I should go there first. Lidie needed me too, and François had never been nice to me. It just seemed right. I hesitated before the door. What if he just yelled at me like always and called me a *prolé*. He didn't deserve the cherries. But I thought of Tomas. He loved his brother, as much as I loved my sister. So, it was for Tomas I was doing this. I took a deep, steadying breath and knocked on the door. Madame Lefévre opened it.

"Do you have a bowl? I brought some cherries for you to give François. They will help him feel better."

"Oh Etienne!" Tomas ran over and embraced me. "Thank you."

I looked over at François lying in the bed. He looked so frail, as if he had been an invalid his entire life. I walked over to the bed and leaned over to whisper into his ear. "François, I suppose we can never be friends, but I want you to know that … I sincerely want you to get better."

I straightened and turned to leave. "Remember, Tomas, you must remove the pits, before feeding him the cherries, or he will choke."

"I will. Thank you, Etienne!"

Tomas hugged me tightly. I smiled at him and broke free of his grasp. I placed half of the cherries in the bowl Madam Lefévre offered. I noticed that she had been crying. I turned to go and ran down to my family's quarters.

Papa met me at the door when I arrived.

"You went to shore, didn't you?" His face was red with anger, and his hands were trembling, but his voice, low and with measured gruffness, spoke with controlled fury.

"Yes, Sir."

"You disobeyed me and the captain! What am I to do with you?" It was not a question he expected me to answer.

"I brought back cherries, for Lidie."

"I told you that God would provide." Papa stepped toward me raising a large, calloused hand.

Maman walked up and put a delicate hand on his arm.

"Maybe God has provided." It was almost a whisper.

Papa turned and looked at her. She stepped between us and stared at my father with her chin held high.

I held my breath and felt my heart thumping in my chest.

Finally, Papa's shoulders relaxed. He gently put a hand on her shoulder and rested his forehead against hers. She wrapped her arms around his neck and whispered into his ear. I didn't know what had just happened, except that, somehow, *Maman* had saved me from my father's anger.

I crossed to Lidie's bed and pulled my knife out of its sheath. I carefully cut out the pits and cut up the cherries into small pieces. I fed them to Lidie one by one. It was difficult, as first. She fought against it. Slowly, she opened her eyes and took a cherry, chewed slowly, and finally, swallowed.

"Louis said you'd come back."

"Did he?"

"Yes. He sat by me while you were gone."

I felt the tears burning my eyes and focused on feeding the cherries to her.

"Louis says it wasn't your fault, but that he is okay. You shouldn't blame yourself anymore."

I was crying in earnest now. Lidie wrapped her arms around my neck. I sobbed into her shoulder. I couldn't stop. I felt Papa's hand on my back.

"It is okay now. Tomorrow is a new day, and everything will be alright."

Maybe this time it really would be.

Epilogue

September 20, 1662

The *St. Jan Baptiste* arrived in port eight days after *De Gilded Bever*, having survived the breakers off the Moray Firth. By then, my father had rented a small room above a tavern in town. Papa and I worked hard those first six months taking whatever odd jobs we could find to pay back our passage. We kept working until, finally, a year ago to the day, we had enough money to purchase a few acres of land.

Living above the tavern those first few months were hard on *Maman.* One day she announced that it was time we found some other place to live. She said that she refused to raise Lidie and Mary so near the great numbers of sailors, pirates and other debauched men that frequented the taverns and pubs each night. So, my father purchased some land to the north of New Amsterdam in an area the Dutch called, *Nieuw Haarlem.* The land was rich with trees and animals.

That Spring we camped out in a tent, while we cleared a large area for a vegetable garden. My father and I then spent the summer felling trees and cutting them into beams and planks to use in building a more permanent house. The large rocks we dug out of the fields we saved for the chimney and stove. *Maman* tended to the cow, the few chickens we were able to acquire, and the vegetable garden. After bringing in the harvest, we started to build our house, in hopes of getting it finished before the winter set in.

We befriended the local Montaukett Indians, who were eager to trade furs for iron hatchets, guns and ammunition, and rum. The Lenape boys taught me to hunt, using a bow I made myself. I had come to New Amsterdam to sell the beaver pelts we obtained from the Lenape and to use the proceeds to buy supplies. I walked toward the business district and entered the fur merchant's shop. The building was near the docks. It had been built of red bricks and embellished in yellow brick from Holland with a red tiled roof and a wooden sign in the shape of a beaver hanging over the front door. A bell tinkled as I entered. My moccasins hardly made a sound on the wood plank floor. I walked to the counter and set my bundle of pelts down and waited.

"Hello, Etienne. It's nice to see you again," Tomas said as he entered the room through the door at the back. "Papa is down at the docks arranging for a ship to carry our pelts to France. What have you brought us?"

"Six beaver pelts and two foxes."

Tomas inspected them and counted out the appropriate number of *wampum* beads in payment. "*Maman* told me to tell you, if I saw you, that she loves the stove you and your father built for us. She wanted me to thank you and your *père* for her. It makes her feel more at home here."

"Thank you. I'll tell him." I took the wampum beads and left the shop. I hurried toward the center of town and entered the general store, where I purchased 20 pounds of flour, 10 pounds of sugar, a jug of rum for Papa, a new saw blade, and a bolt of cloth for *Maman*. I put the rum, sugar, and flour in my pack and, after wrapping the saw blade in butcher paper, strapped it and the cloth to my pack. I stuffed the remaining beads in my pocket and started the three-hour walk back home.

As I approached our home, I saw the smoke rising from our birch bark shelter. Papa was using the axe to make the lintels for the top of the door and windows. I noticed that he had squared up sufficient logs to complete another few rows of planking. Already the walls rose nearly to the top of the doorway.

"I brought a new saw blade, Papa."

Père nodded. "I'm glad they had one. Any troubles?'

"No," I said, showing him my purchases. He nodded, and I handed him the remaining beads.

"So much left? You did well, *Garçon*." Papa stopped his work and studied me. I felt his eyes boring into me. I had never seen that look from him before. It was like he had never seen me before.

"Do you need help with anything?" I asked, breaking the awkward silence.

"No. You have earned a break. Tomorrow we will fit the lintels and finish the walls. Then we can start on the roof. I want to move your mother into this house as soon as possible. Go, take some time for yourself," he said, with a sly smile.

"Thank you, Papa! Tell *Maman* that I will be home for supper." I deposited the flour, sugar, and rum into the storehouse out behind our future kitchen.

Then I cut across the fields, quickening my pace as I approached the forest. The dappled shade was soothing, and I settled into a comfortable stride. My hand instinctively touched my knife. It was still securely fixed to my wampum belt, which was made of finely carved shell beads of white and purple. I found a deer path and followed it down to the river. I crossed the river over a fallen log and continued on until the trees began to thin out again. There on the edge of the woods was a large rock overlooking the Hudson River. I often came to visit this place. I sat and looked out over the water and to the wilderness beyond.

After a time, I heard a faint rustle. I smiled. I knew she would come. Alsoomse slipped onto the rock beside me and, together, we watched as the sun slide toward the horizon.

THE END

In **Book 2,** *A Home in the Wilderness,* Etienne must learn to survive in a dangerous and exotic new world. But just as everything seems to be going well, conflict threatens to destroy it all!

Read on for a preview of Chapter 1.

A Home in the Wilderness is now available on Amazon at
Home-Wilderness-Amanda-Cetas
or wherever books are sold.

Join Amanda M. Cetas' author newsletter and receive updates on future books.at www.amandamcetas.com

New and Foreign Words

Maman – (French) mother or mama

Père – (French) father

Grandpère – (French) grandfather

Garçon – (French) boy or servant

Bèbè – (French) baby

Maitre – (French) Schoolmaster

Oui – (French) yes

Prolé – (French) Abbreviation of *proletariat*, which is a reference to the working class, the lowest social class in France. It was used in a derogatory manner.

Huguenots – Term used for Calvinist Protestant Christians in France

Heresy – a belief that goes against the established beliefs of a religious group or institution

Papist – a derogatory term referring to a Roman Catholic

Cyphering – the term used to refer to performing mathematics

Catechism – religious teachings

Edict - law

Christening – a Christian ceremony signifying spiritual cleansing and rebirth, or baptism

Disavow – deny any responsibility or support for something.

Calvinists – an adherent of the Protestant theological system of John Calvin and his successors.

Curfew – a regulation requiring people to remain indoors between specified hours.

Meester – (Dutch) Mister

Het plezier is van mij – (Dutch) "It is my pleasure."

Pannekoeken – (Dutch) pancake

Ja – (Dutch) yes

Niet mijn vader – (Dutch) "Not my father"

Bos'n' – abbreviation of boatswain; a petty officer on a merchant ship who controls the work of other seamen.

Fo'c'sle – the forward part of a ship below the deck, traditionally used for the crew's living quarters.

Meneer – (Dutch) "I can"

Ballast – heavy weights placed in the bottom of a ship to keep it lover in the water and therefore more stable.

Doctrine – the important, defining beliefs of a religious group.

Blasphemy – the practice of swearing in the name of God.

Posse – a group of people, typically armed, summoned by a sheriff to enforce the law.

Rigging – the ropes used to support a ship's masts and to control or set the sails.

Accost – to confront another

Consoled – to try to make someone feel better.

Jibing – uttering taunting words.

Nautical – a term used to refer to things related to the sea.

Disembark – to get off a ship.

Midshipman – an officer of lowest rank in a navy.

Radial – of or arranged like rays of a circle; diverging lines from a common center.

Quays – a concrete, stone, or metal platform lying alongside or projecting into water for loading and unloading ships.

Couche - diaper

Bourgeoisie – Middle class of society, often the business class

Almshouse – a charity house used to help poor people

Poultice – a moist, mass of material, typically of plant matter, applied to the body to relieve soreness and swelling and kept in place with a cloth.

Hospice – a home providing care for the sick or terminally ill

Requisitions – an official order laying claim to the use of property or materials

Nefarious – wicked or criminal

Indentured Servitude – a position in which a person is required to work for a master for a period of time in order to repay a debt.

Harpsichord – a musical instrument played by means of a keyboard, similar to a piano, but smaller.

Burgermeister – "Master of citizens" this title is given to the chairman of the executive council in many towns and cities in Germanic and Dutch countries.

Corsairs - a term referring to pirates

Moorings – A permanent structure to which a ship may be secured.

Latrines – toilet

Infernal – relating to or characteristic of hell or the underworld.

Cauterized – to stop a wound from bleeding by using high heat to seal the skin.

Decorum – behaving in keeping with good taste and propriety.

Ebony – very dark brown

Constable – a peace officer with limited policing authority, typically in a small town.

Magistrate – A justice of the peace; a judicial office of a lower court.

Quarantined – Restricting the movement of people, isolating them, in order to prevent the spread of disease.

Debauched – indulging in activities of an immoral or harmful nature.

Lintels – the horizontal support across a door or window.

Note to My Readers

The Protestant Reformation began in the early 16th century. Religious thinkers such as, Martin Luther, John Calvin, and Huldrych Zwingli called for a reform of the Catholic Church, ultimately breaking away to form their own Protestant churches. This led to the Wars of Religion that began throughout Europe in the late 16th century. In France, the Huguenots, Protestant followers of John Calvin, fought for their civil rights. In 1598, King Henry IV signed the Edit of Nantes, granting them the freedom to worship in their own way and ending the Wars of Religion in France.

Later, Louis XIII regarded the Huguenots as a threat to his monarchy and worked to eliminate all of their communities in France. Protestant freedoms were restricted and in 1622, the Crown began another series of Huguenot Wars that ended with the Siege of La Rochelle, which lasted 14 months from 1627 through 1628. In 1643, his son, Louis XIV, assumed the throne and in 1660 he married the daughter of the King of Spain, Marie-Thérèse, to seal an alliance with Spain. She was a devout Catholic, and, with her encouragement, Louis XIV declared the beliefs of the Protestants heretical. As part of his plan to reform France and acquire absolute power over his subjects, he issued policies to repress the Protestant Reformed Church in France. These measures forced many Huguenots into hiding while others fled to Amsterdam in October of 1660. Later, they continued their journey to the colony of New Netherlands (present day New

York) in May of 1661.

Over time, Louis XIV deemed this policy insufficient, and he resorted to force, relying on his "dragonnades" and forced lodging of soldiers in Protestant homes. They had the freedom to loot and bully Protestants in order to "encourage" them to recant their heresy and return to the Catholic faith. Then in 1685, Louis XIV issued the Edict of Fontainebleau, which revoked the Edict of Nantes.

Etienne Gayneau and his family were real people, as were many others described in this story. The major events are true as described in the family genealogies, town records, and ship logs I have been able to uncover. For the purposes of this story, I did make Etienne two years older than he had been during the flight from La Rochelle, so that my readers could better identify with him, and so that I could give him more agency. It is important to note, that much responsibility was put on children during this time period, and so they grew up much faster than our children do today.

The scene in which Etienne gathered cherries from Captain Carteret's home on Manhattan, was also true, as recorded in the histories of the *Harlem Its Origin and Early Annals*, though it took place years later, after the family had been living in Harlem awhile. However, the scene seemed an excellent way for Etienne to save his sister and was too fascinating to leave out of the story, and, so, I hope the readers and historical purists will forgive me this indulgence.

The Trip from La Rochelle to Texel and Amsterdam
Western Europe in year 1700 "Courtesy of the University of Texas Libraries,
The University of Texas at Austin."

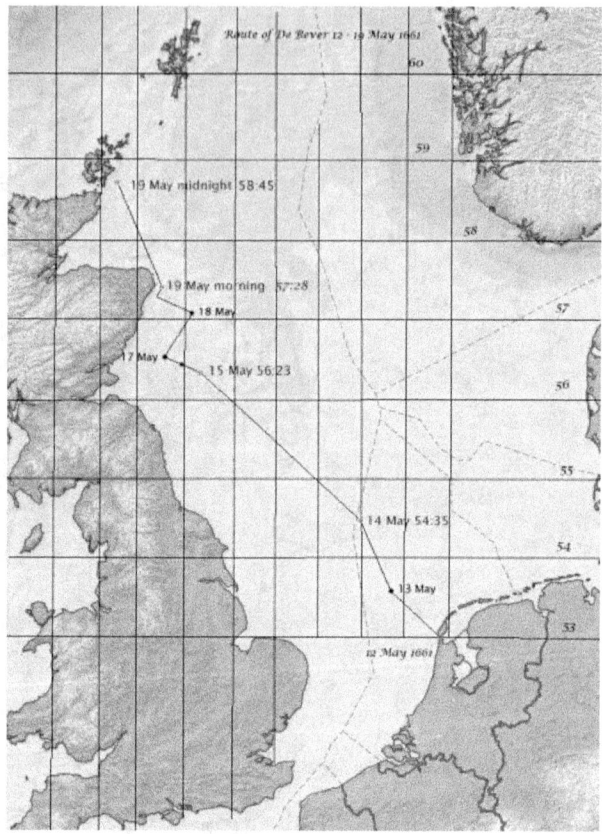

The Trip from Texel to Staten Island Begins
The Vanderhoof Family History Project

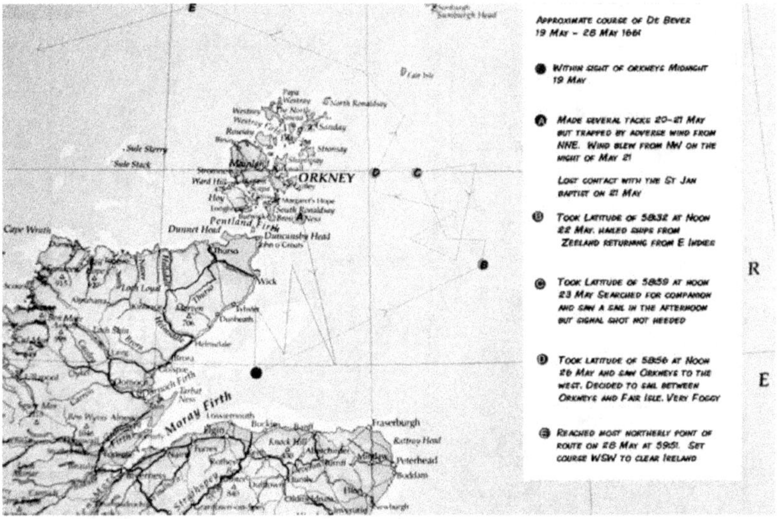
APPROXIMATE COURSE OF DE BEVER
19 MAY - 28 MAY 1661
WITHIN SIGHT OF ORKNEYS MIDNIGHT 19 MAY
A MADE SEVERAL TACKS 20-21 MAY BUT TRAPPED BY ADVERSE WIND FROM NNE. WIND BLEW FROM NW ON THE NIGHT OF MAY 21
LOST CONTACT WITH THE ST JAN BAPTIST ON 21 MAY
B TOOK LATITUDE OF 58.32 AT NOON 22 MAY. HAILED SHIPS FROM ZEELAND RETURNING FROM E INDIES
C TOOK LATITUDE OF 58.59 AT NOON 23 MAY SEARCHED FOR COMPANION AND SAW A SAIL IN THE AFTERNOON BUT SIGNAL SHOT NOT HEEDED
D TOOK LATITUDE OF 58.56 AT NOON 26 MAY AND SAW ORKNEYS TO THE WEST. DECIDED TO SAIL BETWEEN ORKNEYS AND FAIR ISLE. VERY FOGGY
E REACHED MOST NORTHERLY POINT OF ROUTE ON 28 MAY AT 59.51. SET COURSE WSW TO CLEAR IRELAND
ORKNEY
Pentland Firth
Moray Firth
Cape Wrath
Dunnet Head
Duncansby Head
Wick
Thurso
Fraserburgh
Peterhead
Mainland
Hoy
North Ronaldsay
South Ronaldsay
Sanday
Stronsay
Westray
Papa Westray
Sule Skerry
Sule Stack
Sumburgh Head
Fair Isle
Lossiemouth
Banff
Buckie
Rattray Head

The Second Leg of the Trip
The Vanderhoof Family History Project

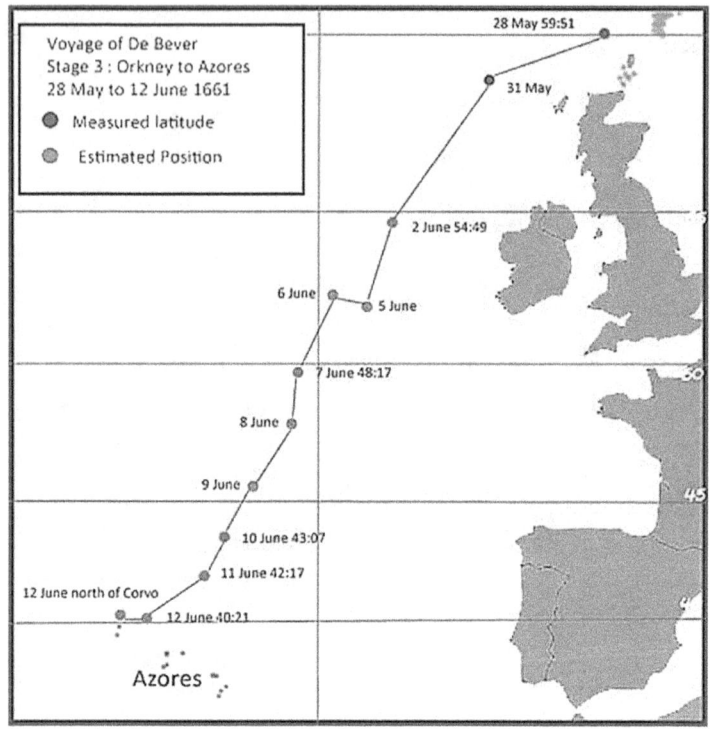

The Third Leg of the Trip
The Vanderhoof Family History Project

Discussion Questions

1. How did Etienne's mother change throughout the book (she seems to start off weak but eventually stands up for her son)? Why was she so weak, after showing strength in leaving her family to marry Etienne's father? How did Etienne's mother and father help/balance each other?

2. What do you think turned François into a bully? How did Etienne deal with it in the end? What did he see between François and François' brother, Tomas? What was their relationship like? Why did they seem so different?

3. Is disobedience for a good cause justified? Etienne left the ship despite the fact that he would be disobeying both his father and the ship's captain. Was this right? Why or why not?

4. What difficulties and anxieties might Etienne face or has he faced in moving to a new country without knowing anything about it? How has he tried to make a new life for himself? How might Etienne's story connect to the immigrant story today?

5. Why do you think there was such animosity between the Huguenots (Calvinist Protestants) and the Catholics? Even the French Huguenots and English Puritans (Reformists), after having left their homelands in order to escape religious persecution, both ended up leaving the Netherlands and

going to America because they felt that there was too much religious tolerance. Does this make them hypocritical? Why or why not?

6. How does the religious persecution in this book relate to today? How do you think they reconciled intolerance of other beliefs even after experiencing persecution them-selves? Do we see the same issues in our society today? What does this say about humanity?

7. Looking at your answers to the questions above, what should be our response to people with differing belief systems?

Acknowledgments

This book is the culmination of three decades of research into my family genealogy and the various court records, ship logs, newspaper articles, land grants, marriage, birth and christening records, in addition to many other primary and secondary sources. I have used numerous invaluable sources over the time it has taken to write this story. However, I would like to acknowledge a few of the most essential sources.

The Vanderhoof Family Project provided invaluable information on the voyage of the *De Bever*, including the ship's journal in English translation, passage rosters, and indentured amounts, maps, and other valuable information. Len Tantillo's research and artwork into the landscape of Manhattan and the surrounding area in the 17th century allowed me to see what Etienne must have seen when he first arrived in New Amsterdam. I would also like to thank him for granting me permission to use his artwork *Manhattan, 1660*.

I would also like to acknowledge the Rijksmuseum, Amsterdam for granting permission to use the two images by Hendrick Cornelisz Vroom entitled, *Return to Amsterdam of the Second Expedition to the East Indies* (1599) and *De Vergulde Bever (The Gilded Beaver)* (1660) and the image by Willem Van de Velde the Younger entitled, *A Ship on the High Seas Caught by a Squall*, known as *"The Gust"* (1680). I would also like to thank the University of Texas for granting the use of their map *Western Europe in year 1700* and the Yorck Project for the use of *La Rochelle, The Harbour Entrance* by Jean Baptist Camille Corot.

Marcus Flynn provided invaluable information and images on the little known potager's stoves built by the French stove makers in the 17th century. I would also like to thank him for the use of his photograph, "The Potager's Stove," *Les Potegers* image, which I converted to a sketch.

Many thanks to Theoden Humphrey for taking the time to read an earlier draft and then in providing his feedback. It meant a lot and helped me see how I could improve some of the weaknesses.

I would like to thank Adriana King, from Fantastic Literary Services, for her invaluable advice and editing services without which this book would not have been fit for publication. Finally, I would like to acknowledge my family for their encouragement along the way, and especially, my husband, Chris, for his unending patience as I filled the house with reference materials while spending hours researching and writing this story.

A Home in the Wilderness

Chapter 1

Unwelcome News

August 11, 1663

I stood on top of the hill and stared down over the smoking wreckage. The remains of so many homes sat smoldering in sad little heaps scattered across the small clearing. The scent of smoke and ash wafted up with the breeze, filling my lungs and making them burn. The only sounds were the low crackling of still-burning wood and a soft child-like wail. I was too late, and Alsoomse had paid the price.

June 10, 1663

I was late and *Maman* was going to kill me.

I cut across the wild pasture, my breath rough. The heavy seed heads of the tall grass all around me, normally bent over as if in prayer, waved in the wind as though sneaking glances at the boy who dared to disturb their sanctuary. A flock of grouse exploded out of the grass ahead of me in a frenzy of feathers and squawking, causing me to jump back in surprise. As my heart pounded, I scanned the horizon ahead. Several cows grazed lazily, their noses buried beneath the sea of green, their tails swishing back and forth in time to music only they could hear. The pasture gave way to fields of waist-high corn and wheat surrounded by split-rail fencing to keep the cows out. I ran toward the fence closest to me and climbed over the railing. I sprinted between the rows of corn until I reached the other side, vaulted over the railing without stopping, and kept running toward town.

I had woken up that morning grumpy and irritable. Nightmares had been plaguing my sleep all week. So, when I'd woken up to our newest brother's piercing shriek after a particularly bad dream about my parents and siblings trapped inside a house on fire, while I stood outside, holding a torch and unable to move … I had not reacted as I should. I was too rough when I changed the baby's clout, making him cry harder. For a moment, all I wanted was to shake him until he was quiet. Instead, I plopped him into the high chair, snapped something at Lidie, and, with the excuse of checking my snares, left the house before anyone could stop me, slamming the door as I left.

The cool morning had helped to clear my head, and I'd relished the excuse to escape my younger siblings. The primitive wilderness of the forest always excited my longing for adventure, almost as much as the sea had. I wasn't sure how long I'd been out, but when I came back with two rabbits for *Maman,* the sun was high in the sky. I'd skinned the hares, cleaned them, and hung them in the smokehouse to cure. Only then did I realize how quiet the house was. Where had everyone gone? That's when I'd remembered the wedding. My family must have already left to meet the procession. I quickly cleaned up, changed into my best Sunday clothes, and took off at a sprint.

Now, as I reached the edge of the village of New Harlem and ran east down a narrow dirt lane, I knew I was in trouble. When the road forked, I took the left-hand road that cut northeast until it bent around due east again. It was called the Great Way because it served as the town's main street. Up ahead, I saw the road that headed north at the Church Farm, a forlorn and neglected plot of farmland reserved for the poor, and, just past it, a cluster of people lined the road. Jacques Cousseau motioned for me to hurry and stand next to him. I slipped into line between him and Jean Guenon. Jacques and Jean had fled La Rochelle with their families at the same time my family had. We'd not been friends until recently though.

I took hold of the white ribbon Jean offered me. Children lined the street on each side with the smallest in front followed by older siblings and finally adults at the back. Jacques, Jean, and I stood behind the children and in front of the adults. Lines of ribbon were strung between the two rows as we waited for the arrival of *le cortège*, the procession. On the opposite side from us and down with the rest of the adults stood my mother resting baby Jeremiah on her now swollen belly, heavy with another forthcoming sibling. She stood beside Papa and both of them glared disapprovingly at me. I shrugged in apology.

I looked back at Jacques, and he smiled sympathetically. The wind started to pick up and pull my hair out of the tie that held it at the nape of my neck. Dark brown curly hair whipped at my face and tickled my nose. I tried to tuck it back behind my ear, but to no avail. I had just put the end of the ribbon between my teeth, so I could use both hands to fix my hair when Jean motioned me to stop.

I looked down the road and saw *le cortège* approaching. Jean Mousnier de la Montagna, the schout, or deputy sheriff of our village, and John Terbosh led the procession. Behind them came their two brides, Maria and Rachel Vermilye, escorted by their father. The rest of their family followed. The Vermilye family were newly arrived from France. It seemed that the religious persecution there had continued to worsen since we'd left.

The procession stopped when it reached the first ribbon. The grooms parted and together the brides cut each ribbon as they slowly moved between the rows of children. Once through the obstacles, the procession made its way to the church where the double ceremony would be held.

The brides and grooms entered the church with the minister and their close family to conduct the ceremony, while the rest of us waited outside talking in hushed voices to friends and family. The church stood on the east side of town between the Harlem River and the Townhall. It was a simple wooden church, painted in white, much like the townhall building, except for the tall, pointed bell tower rising above the front entrance.

Tables had been set up in the Gardens, the common pasture beside the Townhall. The tables had been laid out with roasted turkey and pheasant, boiled carrots and greens. In the middle of the center table stood the *croquembouche*, a large pyramid of dainty round pastries covered in caramel glaze and spun sugar. I had not seen a delicacy such as this, since we had left Amsterdam nearly three years ago. My mouth watered just thinking about it.

A short time later, the two couples and their families emerged from the church to a round of applause. Those men closest to the grooms slapped them happily on the back, while the women spoke quiet words of congratulations to the beaming wives. Jean, Jacques, and I started following the procession out to the gardens when a sharp look from my father stopped me up short. I told Jean and Jacques that I would catch up to them and walked over to my parents.

Maman was in tears, though I couldn't tell if they were happy or sad. Papa looked sternly at me, though I knew that in just a moment he would be laughing with the other adults.

"*Garçon*, your mother and I are disappointed in you and your behavior today. You are not a child anymore, and soon…" *Maman* put a hand on Papa's arm and he paused. "Times will not always be as they are now. Soon you will have to bear a man's responsibilities."

"Let us not spoil this happy day, Husband. There will be time to discuss this further." Papa nodded, clapped a hand on my shoulder. He looked sad, but then he smiled and gestured for me to run along.

The guests were starting to take their seats, and I had just sat down next to Jacques, when a rider galloped up and reigned to a halt near the head table. The man looked a terrible mess, with hair flying, hat askew, and filthy clothes. He looked as though he'd been traveling for days. He approached Schout Montagna and swept the stained hat from his head.

"Sorry to interrupt your wedding, sir, but I have news," the man said, between great gasps of air.

"Come, sit. Take some mead and calm yourself, good man. Then you can tell me your news."

"My pardons, sir. There is no time. I must continue on to New Amsterdam directly. I've just come from our settlement at Wiltwyck. The Indians have completely destroyed the village of *Nieu Dorp* and have attacked Wiltwyck. They have set fire to the houses and have kidnapped several women, including your sister, sir."

The Schout stood abruptly, all signs of joyous celebration wiped out of his demeanor and replaced with the decisive energy that made him New Harlem's leader. "When did this happen?"

"Three days ago. I came directly from there to inform you and the Director."

"I thank you for your haste. Come."

Together the men moved toward the townhall building. An Indian attack, on the mainland... All of my dealings with the native tribes had been good. Alsoomse's people traded beaver furs and otter skins for household goods, guns, and ammunition. They had taught us how to grow corn, beans and squash. I had been fishing and trapping with her brother, Kitchi, many times. He had even shown me how to make snares and a deadfall trap, though I was still trying to get the balance right.

Then the Schout and the messenger returned, beckoning to one of the men nearby.

"Fetch some ale and food for this man before he departs," the Schout said. Then he turned to address the gathering, "We must assemble the elders and discuss our response."

"But Husband, we are only just wed," Maria said, clutching at his hand. The Schout did not even look at his new wife, though he did give her hand a small, comforting pat.

Men all around jumped to their feet and started talking all at once.

"Men of New Harlem steady yourselves!"

The cacophony stilled at once as everyone gave their attention to the Schout. "The savages have taken my sister and several other women and children hostage. They've had at least three or four days to disappear into the forest. And it will take us another four days at least to reach the afflicted town. By then, the savages will likely have fled deep into the mountains. It will be no small task to get there, let alone find them. I have been assured that the men of Wiltwyck are already organizing search parties. Action is needed but planning is too."

Just then the man returned with a skin of ale and a small satchel of food. The Schout nodded to him and turning to the messenger, he said, "Thank you for your notice. Take these provisions to aid you in your journey."

"Thank you, sir!" The messenger sprang onto his horse, reigned it around and headed south down the main road.

The Schout turned back to address the crowd. "My friends, please stay and enjoy yourselves. If the church elders could join me in the townhall, we will discuss our options." He turned and, leaving his bride, headed toward the steps of the townhall followed by five older men with solemn faces.

Men were standing and moving into groups all around the commons. One of these groups had formed near Jean, Jacques, and I.

"I don't see what there is to talk about. We need to go after those savages!" the first man said.

"The attack was way up north, on the outskirts of the colony. There's no immediate danger to us, and the men up there will likely have it resolved before we could mount a response," a stout man replied.

"If the Indians can attack in one place, they can easily attack somewhere else. They are living throughout the colony. We need to make sure they can't harm our families," a third man commented.

"And how do you propose we do that?" the stout man asked.

"We need to raise the militia and eliminate the threat!" the first man exclaimed.

Raising the militia? That would not be good. I thought of Alsoomse. It couldn't have been her tribe, but would the townsfolk even care?

Fear had a way of making men target anyone different from them, even if they weren't at fault. I had learned that lesson in La Rochelle, when we had been the targets of Catholic fear and intolerance. I had to find Alsoomse and warn her! I quickly excused myself and moved toward the road.

"Etienne, where are you going?" *Maman* had come up behind me and caught my arm.

I explained my fears and looked into her blue eyes pleadingly.

"Be careful, and be swift," she said, releasing me.

There was silence when I reached Alsoomse's village. Every year her tribe would migrate up north to their winter camp. But it was summer now. They should have been back weeks ago. There should have been women bustling around preparing dinner and men sitting by the fire sharing stories, but instead there was silence.

I entered the village and walked from house to house, looking for any sign or clue that might explain their absence. I took one more look through the village, knowing it was pointless, and paused at the house where Alsoomse's family lived. It was dark inside.

I sat down on the bare platforms that served as their beds. I sat there for a long time. The moon rose, and I watched its silvery light sliding across the ground, creating strange illusions of snakes or rats swarming over the ground. Just then something glinted off the ground near the doorway. I reached down and picked up a small strand of wampum, fingering it gently. Where *were* they?

I sighed and rose, slowly, to go home. *Please God, keep them safe.*

About the Author

Photo by Jim Irish, 2019

Amanda M. Cetas is the author of the historical adventure *Thrown to the Wind*, which is the first book in the series, *A Country for Castoffs*. The story is taken from her family history, which she has spent over two decades researching. She currently teaches several courses in American, European and World history to advanced high school students. She also taught at the middle school level for several years.

Amanda lives in Tucson, Arizona for most of the year with her husband and two little Yorkie mixes. She escapes to the beach at Rocky Point, Mexico over every break in the school year and to the Willamette River in Portland, Oregon each summer. She has three grown children and two beautiful grandchildren.

Visit her website at Amanda M. Cetas, Writer to connect with her and join her mailing list or follow her on Facebook, Instagram, BookBub, or GoodReads.

Amanda M. Cetas